Love
Calling

Janet Lee Barton

D1561397

Heartsong Presents

To Dan, my biggest encourager, I love you.
And
To my Lord and Savior for showing me the way.

A note from the Author:

I love to hear from my readers! You may correspond with me by writing:

Janet Lee Barton
Author Relations
P.O. Box 9048
Buffalo, NY 14240-9048

ISBN-13: 978-0-373-48651-9

LOVE CALLING

This edition issued by special arrangement with Barbour Publishing, Inc., 1810 Barbour Drive, Uhrichsville, Ohio, U.S.A.

Chapter 1

New York City, Fall 1898

Emma Chapman stepped off the trolley and began walking the few blocks home. *Home*. Not the orphanage, but a real home. She still couldn't believe she lived in this neighborhood filled with beautiful brownstone town houses. Still couldn't believe she had a paying position as a telephone operator at the New York Telephone Company.

She'd applied in July and began training the very next day. It hadn't been easy, not with a supervisor over her shoulder for weeks on end, but finally she'd been assigned her own switchboard with about two hundred lines to care for.

She'd just begun to realize that most of the other girls would have given anything to have her bank of lines. Evidently the girl before her had left to be married, and the telephone company didn't like to switch operators once their customers got used to them. It was too stressful for the customers to get to know someone else, so Emma had wound up serving many of the wealthy families in the city.

It took awhile for her to fully comprehend it, but once she finally recognized that she was actually speaking to *the* Mrs. Margaret Vanderbilt nearly every day, she was momentarily tongue-tied, causing the woman to ask, "Operator? Operator! Are you there?"

"Yes ma'am. I'm sorry. I'm a bit new, but I'm right here. Whom may I connect you to?"

Mrs. Vanderbilt had been very gracious once she found out Emma was the new operator—evidently the girl Emma replaced had mentioned that she'd be leaving to get married—and she'd insisted on knowing Emma's name. "I like to be on friendly terms with the operators. The two young men who work nights and weekends are quite amicable, but I don't converse with them that much. I'm sure we'll get along just fine, Emma. Now please ring me through to Lord & Taylor department store. They sent out the right order, but I asked for the wrong size, and I must get it all sorted out."

"Yes ma'am," Emma had said, before quickly connecting the Vanderbilt line with Lord & Taylor.

Emma knew the operators weren't to listen in on conversations, but the customers could talk to them anytime they wanted. And many did, wanting to know all manner of things. It turned out that Mrs. Vanderbilt did like to converse from time to time. Emma wasn't sure what would happen if her supervisor found her talking to the woman, but Emma decided she'd let her talk to Mrs. Vanderbilt and tell *her* not to talk to the operators.

Now as she neared home, Emma counted her blessings, for she had many more now than she'd had a few months ago. She hurried up the steps to Mrs. Holloway's house,

"Sam, I'm sorry we weren't down before you got here," Emma said. She looked quite lovely tonight in a summery pink-and-green floral dress.

"We dillydallied the afternoon away and were late changing," Grace informed him.

"You all look quite nice, so it was worth the wait," Sam said.

"Oh, you always say the nicest things, doesn't he, Emma?" Grace said. "If I were a little older—"

"Grace Chapman!" Emma said, shaking her head.

Grace laughed. "Oh, he knows I'm teasing, Emma. Don't you, Sam?"

"I do. And I'm sure that I seem quite old to Grace. Probably even to you, Emma. But if I were a little younger. . ."

Everyone chuckled at his comeback, and as Sam watched Emma blush a delicate shade of pink, he felt his own neck grow warm. Now why had he said that? He'd made up his mind not to let himself become overly attracted to another woman, and he was determined to follow through with his decision. He never wanted to lose another woman he loved, and the only way to avoid that was to not fall in love.

JANET LEE BARTON

has lived all over the southern United States, but she and her husband plan to now stay put in Oklahoma. With three daughters and six grandchildren between them, they feel blessed to have at least one daughter and her family living in the same town. Janet loves being able to share her faith through her writing. Happily married to her very own hero, she is ever thankful that the Lord brought Dan into her life, and she wants to write stories that show that the love between a man and a woman is at its best when the relationship is built with God at the center. She's very happy that the kind of romances the Lord has called her to write can be read by and shared with women of all ages, from teenagers to grandmothers alike.

Books by Janet Lee Barton

HEARTSONG PRESENTS

HP434—*Family Circle*
HP532—*A Promise Made*
HP562—*Family Ties*
HP623—*A Place Called Home*
HP644—*Making Amends*
HP689—*Unforgettable*
HP710—*To Love Again*
HP730—*With Open Arms*
HP745—*Family Reunion*

HP759—*Stirring Up Romance*
HP836—*A Love for Keeps*
HP852—*A Love All Her Own*
HP868—*A Love to Cherish*
HP956—*I'd Sooner Have Love*
HP971—*Sooner Sunrise*
HP988—*Sooner Sunset*
HP1032—*Remedy for the Heart*

and as usual, Jones, the butler, opened the door for her. She never had figured out how he knew the exact minute she reached the top step, but he did.

"Good afternoon, Miss Emma. I hope you had a nice day."

"I did, Jones. Thank you. I hope you did, too?"

"I did. You know with all the wedding preparations going on, there isn't a dull day around here lately."

Emma chuckled. "I suppose not. Is Mrs. Holloway in the parlor?"

"She is. I'll bring tea in shortly."

Mrs. Holloway had a practice of serving tea each afternoon about the time Emma and her cousin, Esther, got home from work. Esther was a pharmacist apprentice who would be getting married to Mrs. Holloway's nephew come Christmas.

Emma was thrilled for them. They made a wonderful couple, even if their relationship had been a bit rocky in the beginning. A physician who thought a woman's place was in the home and a woman who'd gone to college to become a pharmacist were bound to clash at first—especially after he found out she was also interested in the women's suffrage movement.

Emma chuckled remembering back to some of their skirmishes. But love prevailed and Andrew's views changed over time. Now he was as big a supporter of the movement as any man she knew.

She entered the parlor and was greeted by her younger sister, Grace, and Mrs. Holloway.

"Good afternoon, Emma, how was your day?" Mrs. Holloway asked.

"It was a good day. It passed very quickly, as usual." That was one of the things she loved best about her job. She stayed so busy time seemed to fly by.

"And did you speak to any of the Vanderbilts today?" soon-to-be fifteen-year-old Grace asked.

"I did. But only for a moment or two."

"Oh, too bad."

Grace loved to hear about her customers.

"What all did you do today? How was school?"

"It was great. You know I love my new high school. Mrs. Holloway said I might ask one of my friends over after school one day soon, if you and Esther don't mind."

"Mrs. Holloway has the final say in those kinds of things around here. You know that."

Her sister grinned. "I do know. But she insists on my asking you two."

"Girls, don't talk about me as if I'm not here. I just believe it's the right thing to do. Although I won't promise not to try to persuade them on occasion if they say no," Mrs. Holloway said in a teasing manner.

The woman had become a mother figure to all of them, even though they'd not known her all that long. She'd been Esther's benefactor, taking her in once she had to leave the orphanage and then sending her to the Philadelphia College of Pharmacy. Then, once Esther came back to do her apprenticeship and it was time for Emma to leave the orphanage, she took both Emma and Grace in. The woman was a true blessing.

"I believe we've all decided you have our best interests at heart, Mrs. Holloway. And truly, if you don't mind if Grace has a friend over now and again, then Esther and I aren't going to object."

"Then you might as well telephone your friend and ask her, Grace," Mrs. Holloway said.

"Thank you, I will." Grace hurried out of the room.

"You're sure you don't mind?" Emma turned to the older woman.

"Oh Emma, I don't mind at all. I love having this home filled with young people. I just wish I'd have had you all from earlier ages. I enjoy every minute I have with you now though, and I'm thankful that Grace is young enough that I'll have her for several years before she thinks seriously of marrying. I don't feel I've had Esther here near long enough, and now she's going to be a married woman in only a matter of months!"

"But, she *is* marrying your nephew," Emma said. "And they'll be living only a few blocks away."

"I know, but that will be two fewer people—"

"Two fewer people for what?" Esther asked as she entered the parlor.

"Mrs. Holloway is going to miss you and Andrew when you move out."

Emma smiled as her cousin hurried over to hug her soon-to-be aunt.

"Oh, you know we'll be over often," Esther said. "You'll probably get tired of us showing up on your doorstep for a meal. I really must learn how to cook, you know."

"You'll be welcome here anytime; you know that."

"Of course we do," Esther said. "We're very thankful for it. And we're here for a few more months, too."

"Only because you helped me talk Andrew into waiting until you both could find a home to suit your needs, and to give us time to plan the wedding you both deserve and that my sister will be happy with."

"Well, we did need to find a place. But I think Andrew's idea for us to turn the upstairs of his office building into a home for us is the right answer for now. It's not far from the pharmacy, and we'll be right there where we both work. It will also give us more time to find a home when we begin to have a family."

They'd all been poring over the plans to turn the top

floors of Andrew's office into a home, and Emma thought it was going to be lovely. They actually could stay there for several years, even if they started a family early. With three bedrooms, she even hoped she and Grace would be able to stay over once in a while. It certainly was going to seem strange to visit her cousin as a married woman. Esther was blessed. Dr. Andrew Radcliff was very much in love with her, as Esther was with him. One could almost feel the love arcing between them when they were in the same room.

Emma dreamed of getting married of course, but she never wanted to settle for anything other than the real kind of love her cousin had found. She was certain it would be worth waiting for. And that was good, because she hadn't met anyone who captured her attention in that way at all.

Sam Tucker wasn't sure why he felt the sudden urge to visit the orphanage where he'd been raised, but he did. Maybe it was because he knew the cop who'd been transferred to this beat and wanted to let Mrs. Robertson and the kids know that they finally had a decent policeman now watching over them.

Or maybe it was because he was lonesome. Whatever the reason, he rang the doorbell of the Ladies Aide Society Orphanage and waited. Mrs. Robertson's assistant answered the door. Her wide face broke into a huge smile when she recognized him. "Samuel Tucker! You're a sight for sore eyes, you are! Come in, come in. Mrs. Robertson is in her office—I assume that's who you've come to see?"

"Yes ma'am, Mrs. Harrison. How have you been?"

"I've been good. Keeping up with the children keeps me going. I heard about your wife. I'm so sorry."

"Thank you." Sam didn't ask how she knew about Ann. But her words comforted him. They'd only been married a few months when Ann had been run over trying to cross Broadway. It'd been just over a year since one of his fellow officers had come to the police station to tell him, but some days it felt like yesterday. This was one of those days.

They reached Mrs. Robertson's office, and Mrs. Harrison motioned for him to stay behind her as she peeked around the door. "Mrs. Robertson?"

"Yes? What is it, Laura?"

"Look who's come to see us." She motioned for Sam to stand beside her.

"Hello, Mrs. Robertson. I hope it's not a bad time. I just wanted to come and—"

The woman who'd raised him from the age of about ten pushed away from her desk to step around to him. "Sam! I was just thinking about you and wondering how you've been. It's a fine time to come visit!" She reached him and threw her arms around him. "It's good to see you, son."

Then Sam knew why he'd come. Something about this woman's presence had always given him comfort from the first day he'd come to live at the orphanage, and evidently he needed her comfort now.

"It's good to see you, too. I've been a bit lonely lately, and I had a sudden urge to come see how everyone is here."

"I'm glad you did. I was about to have Laura make us some tea. Will you have a cup with us? Or she can bring you coffee if you'd rather."

"Tea will be fine. But please, don't go to any trouble for me."

"No trouble at all," Mrs. Harrison said. "I'll be back in a shake."

"Come. Have a seat, Sam." Mrs. Robertson motioned to one of the chairs in front of her desk as she took her own seat.

Sam did as she suggested. Last time he sat in one of

these chairs was the day he left. But he'd been there many times through the years—usually when he was in trouble for one thing or another. But Mrs. Robertson had always been fair, and he'd learned to respect her early on.

"We heard about your wife. I'm so very sorry, Sam. I didn't know where to send a card—"

"That isn't your fault, and I'm sorry. I should have kept in better touch. I guess at first I thought I could leave here and just get on with my life, but I forgot that the people who'd become an important part of my life were right here, and that this place had become home to me over the years."

Mrs. Robertson nodded. "It's that way for most. Only a few realize it from the first. Sadly though, you've been gone long enough that most of those you might remember have also left and begun lives of their own."

Sam nodded. "I know. But you're still here and so is Mrs. Harrison."

"We are. I expect we will be for a while to come."

"I'm glad. For me and for all the children you'll help to raise."

"Enough about me. Tell me how it's going being on the police force."

"You know?"

Mrs. Robertson laughed. "They did do a check on you of sorts, you know. And I can tell you that I gave you a glowing report."

"I suspected as much. And I thank you for it."

"You're welcome. I'm glad Commissioner Roosevelt began cleaning the department up before you decided to become part of it. The corruption was rampant."

Sam nodded. "True. And that's one reason I wanted to become a policeman—to help clean it up. To be at least one on the street that a kid could come up to and learn to trust not to blame them for everything just because they are an—"

"Orphan?"

Sam nodded. "Or living in the tenements, or even on the streets. We have many who do live in those conditions. I don't think most of us raised in an orphanage realized that we had it good."

Mrs. Harrison arrived just then with the tea, and after they'd all been served, she took the other chair beside Sam.

"I was just asking Sam how he liked being on the police force."

"And how glad we are that Mr. Roosevelt is in charge now. How is that going, really?" Mrs. Harrison asked.

"Oh, he's made sweeping changes. But, and I hate to say it, he's made enemies, too. Still, I'm proud to be part of his police force, I can tell you that. And I also can tell you that this area will have a new cop watching over it soon."

"Oh? Are you telling us Officer Ryan will be leaving?"

"I am. He's being replaced by a friend of mine."

"Oh Sam, that is wonderful news! I can't tell you what a relief it will be to be rid of him. He blames everything bad that happens around here on our children."

"I know. I've been the recipient of his pointing finger many times in the past. I'm happy someone more understanding is going to take his place. Over time, maybe some of the kids here will learn we're not all corrupt."

"That'd be a blessing, for sure," Mrs. Robertson said. "Now, let's see…who can I catch you up on? John O'Malley comes by from time to time. He's a teacher now."

"Oh, I'm glad to hear that. He always said that was what he wanted to do. What about George Smith?" He'd had a little bit of the rebel in him, and Sam hoped he'd done well, too.

But Mrs. Robertson shook her head. "George got in

with the wrong people after he left here. Last I heard he was in jail for trying to rob a jewelry store."

"I'm sorry to hear that."

"Yes, we were, too. But Esther Melrose did very well. She's a pharmacist-in-training and lives with her benefactor, Mrs. Holloway. Esther's engaged to be married to Mrs. Holloway's nephew, who is a doctor."

Sam grinned. Esther had always been very kind, looking after her younger cousins and others at the orphanage. She'd been about two years younger than him, and her cousin Emma must have been about four years younger.

"What about her cousins? Emma and…Grace?"

"They're fine. Actually, they are all living with Mrs. Holloway now. Once she found out it was time for Emma to leave the orphanage, and that Esther and Emma were heartsick about leaving Grace, she took them both in. They are all very happy, and they stop by pretty often to see us."

"I'm glad they do. I know they meant a lot to most of the younger girls. What is Emma doing now?"

"She's working for the New York Telephone Company as an operator. She seems to really like it a lot."

"I'd like to see those girls again." Sam wasn't sure why. Maybe it was just a connection to what had been family to him.

"I'm sure they'd love to see you, too. I can give you Mrs. Holloway's address. I know she won't mind you stopping by. She even invited us to Emma's eighteenth birthday party."

"If you're sure they wouldn't mind, I'd love to have the address."

Mrs. Robertson pulled out a sheet of paper and wrote down the address. "Here you go. I'm glad you want to stay in touch, Sam. We've missed you around here."

"I've missed you all, too." More than he'd ever thought

he would. And he was determined to stay in touch from now on. He took the paper from Mrs. Robertson and looked at it. His eyebrow raised a notch. It wasn't all that far from here, but in terms of society, it was a world apart. The girls had done very well for themselves. And he'd be sure to see them sooner or later—their neighborhood was his new beat.

"Don't let the address stop you. Mrs. Holloway is a wonderful woman and will welcome you. In fact, I might just telephone her to let her know you might stop by."

Sam nodded. "That might be best. I'll try to go by today." While Mrs. Robertson's assurance that he'd be welcome remained fresh in his mind and he had enough nerve.

Chapter 2

Keeping his nerve up was something altogether different from having it for a few minutes in the first place, Sam realized as he grabbed a trolley and headed toward the Holloway home. He hadn't mentioned it to Mrs. Robertson, but a few days ago, he'd been almost positive he'd seen Emma Chapman on this same trolley. Then, he'd decided it couldn't have been, because that young woman, even if she'd left the orphanage, would live in a whole different world than the one he'd be patrolling. Still, she'd looked a lot like Emma, only even prettier than he remembered and quite the young lady now. He realized now that most likely, it had been her.

Sam watched the passing landscape, not sure if he was happy to have this fairly wealthy neighborhood as his beat or if he'd have been happier to have the one that included the orphanage. What could really happen here that he'd be needed for? Oh, his supervisor had told him he'd be surprised when he'd asked him the question.

"There are all kinds of crimes, Tucker. Some just aren't as out in the open as others. You'll be busy, I assure you."

Sam certainly hoped so. He wanted to make a difference in this city. The trolley slowed to a stop a few blocks away from the address Mrs. Robertson had given him, and he got off and headed up to the corner and then took a left on the side street. Maybe he should have worn his uniform, but he didn't officially start working the beat until Monday, and he enjoyed wearing regular clothes as often as he could.

He was proud to be a policeman under Commissioner Roosevelt, but there was still much work to do among the force to gain the trust of the people they were to protect. For much too long the corruption in the department had tainted what it was supposed to stand for. It'd been, and would continue to be, a challenge for years to come, but Sam hoped that one day the department would earn the trust it had tried to demand for so long.

Sam glanced down at the paper in his hand and found he was standing right outside the Holloway town house. A nicely kept three-story brownstone, it was far removed from the homes he usually visited—and very much removed from where he'd grown up. Now he stood straight and tall, trying to regain the confidence he'd felt only an hour ago.

He sent up a prayer. *Lord, I really need to connect with some old friends now. You know how lonely I've been since Ann's death. The few friends I've made since leaving the orphanage are married and have started their families, and I feel out of place most of the time. Please let Mrs. Robertson be right and let the girls be glad to see me.*

He reached out his hand to ring the bell and then quickly

lowered it. *Like I'm not going to feel out of place here?*
Sam shook off the discouraging thought. He'd be seeing the
inside of these homes in the future. His first time might as
well be in a home where old friends might welcome him.
He rang the bell.

The door was quickly answered by a portly man he as-
sumed to be a butler. "Good afternoon, sir, what may I
do for you?"

Sam cleared his throat. "I was wondering if Miss Melrose and the Misses Chapman are available for a call?"

"Might I ask who is calling, sir?"

"You may tell them it's Samuel Tucker."

The door opened wider. "Please come in and wait while
I see if they are receiving visitors."

"Thank you." Sam resisted the urge to chuckle. How
things had changed for the girls. At the orphanage, someone would have called out, "Esther, Emma, Grace...Sam
is here to see you!"

But there was no yelling in this home, and he wondered if there ever had been. Yet he was not disappointed
when Esther and her cousins hurried out of the room he
presumed to be the parlor and rushed up to him. A man
followed behind them, and he wondered if he might be
Esther's fiancé.

"Sam Tucker! Is it really you?" Esther asked.

She was as pretty as Sam remembered, but the one that
caught his eye was Emma. She was no longer the child
she'd been when he left the orphanage—nor for that matter was Grace. Now, it was Grace who was around the age
he had been when he left, and Emma...had turned into a
beauty. Her dark hair a cloud around her face, and her eyes
the color of the sky on a cloudless day.

"It is. And I do recognize you, Esther. You're as pretty
as ever."

"Thank you, Sam." She turned to the man who'd moved closer to her. "Andrew, this is an old friend from the orphanage, Sam Tucker. Sam, this is my fiancé, Dr. Andrew Radcliff."

Sam grinned and held out his hand. "Pleased to meet you, Mr. Radcliff. You are a fortunate man."

"Pleased to meet you, too, Mr. Tucker. I am blessed for sure." Andrew smiled down at Esther and then nodded at Emma and Grace. "I can tell from the girls' welcome it's been awhile since they've seen you."

"It has, to my regret. And I'm not sure I would have recognized Emma and Grace if they weren't here with Esther."

Grace giggled, and Emma smiled and said, "It's good to see you haven't changed a bit, Sam. Always something nice to say—at least to us."

"Please join us in the parlor. I'm afraid we all just up and left my aunt presiding over tea."

"Which is about to get cold, I might add." An older woman Sam presumed to be Mrs. Holloway had come out of the parlor and made her way toward them. "Please, do join us, Mr. Tucker. I've heard your name mentioned by the girls. From the looks of it, they've all missed you."

"As I have them," Sam admitted.

"This is Mrs. Holloway, Sam," Emma said. "She's taken us all in and we love her very much."

"Pleased to meet you, ma'am." Sam thought she might be in her fifties, but she was aging so gracefully it was hard to tell how old she might be.

"Thank you. I'm pleased to meet you as well. And any friend of my girls is welcome here."

"That's good to know." Now that he'd connected with them again, he was going to make sure he stayed in contact.

"In fact, I was just about to tell the girls that I'd had a

telephone call from Mrs. Robertson this afternoon telling me that you might be stopping by. I'm glad you did."

"Thank you, ma'am. Mrs. Robertson told me you
wouldn't mind my stopping by."

"Not at all," Mrs. Holloway said.

"Come on, Sam. We have a lot to catch up on," Grace
said, putting a hand through his arm. He looked at Emma,
and she slid her own hand through his other arm.

Mrs. Holloway led the way, with Sam, Emma, and
Grace behind her and Esther and her fiancé following behind.

Emma couldn't believe Sam Tucker had shown up after
all this time. She'd looked up to him when he'd still been
at the orphanage. He'd always kept the other boys in line.
But then he left and never came back to see them, and she'd
been a bit heartbroken over it.

He was even handsomer than she remembered, his dark
auburn hair neat and trim and combed to the side, his
brown eyes reminding her of the fudge they used to talk
Mrs. Robertson into letting them make every once in a
while. She'd heard he'd gotten married. Was he still?

"Please take a seat, Mr. Tucker," Mrs. Holloway said.

He looked around and took a seat on one end of a couch.

"Would you prefer tea or coffee? We have both."

"I'd like coffee, please."

She poured him a cup and handed it to Emma.

"If I remember right, you like your coffee black, no
cream, no sugar?" Emma asked.

"You remember well." He accepted the cup from her
before she took a seat on the other end of the sofa.

Once everyone was settled with their refreshment, Esther turned to Sam. "We heard you'd gotten married, is
that true?"

Sam's smiling demeanor suddenly changed, and Emma saw the sorrow in his eyes.

"I did get married. But…" He stopped and cleared his throat. "My wife was killed in an accident only months after our wedding."

A collective gasp was heard. Tears sprung to Emma's eyes. "Oh Sam, I'm so sorry. I…" She didn't know quite what to say next.

"Please accept our condolences, Mr. Tucker," Mrs. Holloway said. "Losing a mate is tragic, no matter how long one has been married, but especially hard, I would think, when you've just begun your life together."

Sam nodded. "Thank you, ma'am, Emma, and all of you. It hasn't been easy. Ann was a wonderful woman, and I miss her dearly. It's been over a year now, but it still feels like yesterday at times."

"How did—?"

"Grace!" Emma scolded. "I don't believe you asked that."

"It's all right, Emma. I can talk about it now. She was killed trying to cross Broadway. Witnesses said an omnibus came around a corner at breakneck speed, so fast that it turned over and pinned Ann and another person underneath." Sam paused before continuing. "I was told she died right away."

Emma fought back tears. How tragic. And to think they'd only been married such a short time. Her heart broke for him.

"I'm sorry, Sam," Grace said. "I shouldn't have made you think about it again."

Sam smiled and shook his head. "Don't worry, Grace. I would have told you all in time, and I think about it often anyway. But, I didn't come here to make you all sad. I just wanted to catch up with what has been going on in your lives. I can see they've changed quite a bit."

"Oh yes, thanks to Mrs. Holloway, our lives have changed more than we ever thought possible," Emma said.

"It started when Mrs. Holloway offered to be my benefactor and send me to the Philadelphia College of Pharmacy," Esther said.

"I remember you wanted to make medicine so that people didn't have to die like all of your parents did," Sam said.

Emma was struck by how good his memory was. He seemed to remember a lot about them, but then she remembered a lot about him, too. He'd always been one of her favorites, and deep down she remembered having a few girlish daydreams about marrying him one day. Not that she'd ever tell anyone.

"I did," Esther continued. "And Mrs. Holloway made that dream come true. Then, when I came home to start my apprenticeship, she realized that Emma would have to leave the orphanage when she turned eighteen and that would leave Grace alone. We know Mrs. Robertson would have taken good care of her, but the thought of Grace being by herself broke both mine and Emma's hearts."

"And I had no idea what I was going to do," Emma said. "I didn't really want to go to school like Esther, but I had to find a job and a place to live."

"Then Mrs. Holloway answered everyone's prayers by asking us to come live with her," Grace finished.

"That is what Mrs. Robertson told me. What a wonderful thing to do, Mrs. Holloway," Sam said.

"I'm the one who has been blessed by having them here with me, Mr. Tucker. I only wish I'd done it much earlier in their lives."

"And now you see why we love her so much," Emma said.

Sam nodded. "I do. And Esther, how do you like being a pharmacist?"

"I love it, Sam."

"It seems to be the perfect match to Dr. Radcliff's profession."

Everyone laughed, and Sam looked at Emma. "What did I say?"

"It's not you. We're just remembering how it was when they first met. Andrew did not think a woman should be entering what he considered a *man's* field."

"Oh, I see," Sam said.

Emma couldn't help but wonder if he felt the same way about where a woman's place was as the two men exchanged glances. "But he's come around and even defends her choice now."

Andrew grinned and shrugged. "Esther and her cousins helped me see the error of my ways. Many of us hold on to the long-held ideas in our families, but I'm thankful to have parents who can admit when they've been wrong, too."

Emma knew Sam had always been one to speak his mind, and she waited to see if he'd say anything about how blessed Andrew had been to have his parents at all.

But Sam only nodded and took a sip of coffee before turning to Grace. "I assume you are busy with high school. You go to the one a few blocks from here?"

"I do. I've made friends already."

"And Emma, Mrs. Robertson said you work for the New York Telephone Company. How do you like it?"

"I like it very much."

"That's good."

"What about you, Sam? We have no idea what field of work you decided to go into." Emma felt it was time to find out more about him.

"I guess it's time to confess. I'm a policeman. In fact, this is my new beat."

Few things he could have said would have surprised Emma more. "A policeman? Sam, why in the world would you want to be a policeman? We all know how corrupt that department has been."

"*Has* been is right, Emma. But under Commissioner Roosevelt, it started getting cleaned up—and hopefully, that will continue under the new and future superintendents. There's still much to do of course. But those of us who want to see the department be what it should be are willing to work toward making it become one the people of this city can trust."

Emma didn't know what to say. They'd all decried the department when they lived at the orphanage—and Sam's voice was one of the loudest. Her sister and cousin seemed as much at a loss for words as she was.

Finally, it was Mrs. Holloway who spoke. "There has been much change to the department under Commissioner Roosevelt. I'm hopeful that the changes he's implemented will continue under others, and I admire your willingness to help the commissioner improve the department, Mr. Tucker."

Sam looked relieved that the silence had been broken, and Emma felt bad that she'd contributed to his discomfort. She hadn't meant to.

"Thank you, ma'am. I believe I know why the girls are a bit taken aback."

Even in their rudeness, Sam managed to take up for them. He'd always been that way.

"The policemen who patrolled the area around the orphanage were mean men, and we always got blamed for about anything that went wrong. And I didn't have anything good to say about the department either. I can see why they would think it might be the last place I'd be employed."

"The very last place," Esther said.

Sam nodded. "I know. But when I left the orphanage, I wanted to do more than work the docks, and I didn't have any training in much of anything, other than selling papers. I got a job delivering groceries, but I wanted more. Then I found out there were going to be big changes in the police department and decided I wanted to be part of them."

Emma's heart was heavy. All the policemen she'd come into contact with had been bad. In fact, she'd never known a good cop in her life. The corruption in the department ran deep, and she doubted it would ever be eradicated. Oh, she'd heard things were getting cleaned up, but they always said that when someone new was in charge. Only now she prayed it was true—for Sam's sake.

"I wish you the best, Sam," Esther spoke up. "I know the department is fortunate to have you. And please, forgive us for not being more enthused. I'm ashamed of myself. After all, I chose to go into a field few women are even interested in. And I know what it's like to have people against what you feel called to do. You have my total support."

"Thank you, Esther. I appreciate that more than I can say."

"I'm glad our neighborhood is part of your beat. That means we'll see you more often," Grace said.

"It's always good to know the policemen patrolling one's neighborhood, Mr. Tucker. I'm pleased it will be you," Mrs. Holloway said. "You've barely begun to catch up with each other. Why don't you stay and have dinner with us?"

"Oh yes, Sam!" Grace said. "Please do."

"That is a wonderful idea, Mrs. Holloway. Thank you

for suggesting it. Do stay, Sam. I'd like you to get to know Andrew better," Esther said.

"If you're all sure, I'd love to," Sam said.

If he noticed that Emma hadn't added her support, he didn't say so—which made her feel even worse. She hated that he was a cop. It made her feel sick in the pit of her stomach. But Sam was Sam, after all. She forced the words out. "Please do join us, Sam."

Chapter 3

Emma watched Sam leave later that evening and felt horrible for treating him the way she had. He'd suffered so much in losing his wife, and then he'd obviously needed to seek out people he considered friends. Many of the ones who'd been in the orphanage at the same time he had, those who would be the same age, no longer lived in the area.

But as he'd explained during dinner, he'd come to realize that the only family he had were those he'd been raised with and his wife's parents. And she'd let him down. Oh, Emma could hope he hadn't noticed that she'd had little to say to him, but deep down she knew he had. She'd caught him looking her way several times during dinner.

And if she thought Grace and Esther hadn't noticed, she was wrong. They waited only until Sam had gone, Andrew had gone to the hospital to check on a patient, and Mrs. Holloway had headed upstairs, to let her know how they felt.

"Emma, you were downright rude to Sam," Esther chided. "I understand your concern for him, but don't look down on him because he wants to help this city—no matter how much you think it is a lost cause."

"You probably made him feel unwelcome," Grace said. "And I want him to come back. He's always been like a big brother to me, and I've missed him!"

"You certainly didn't throw your support his way at the very first. You were as surprised as I was at his decision."

"But we did come around," Esther said. "You didn't say much of anything to him the rest of the evening."

"Mrs. Holloway and you two made it very clear he's welcome here anytime. Sam will be back," Emma said. She certainly hoped she wouldn't be the cause of him staying away.

"You don't know that," Grace said.

"I'm *sorry*! I just couldn't help it. I didn't know what to say, feeling the way I do. And we haven't seen Sam for several years. How do you know he hasn't…" She couldn't even form the words.

"Changed so much he'll be like all the other policemen we've known?" Esther seemed to know exactly was Emma was thinking.

"Well, we don't know."

"Oh Emma, really now? This is Sam we are talking about. He's a good man. He was always the one who took up for anyone he thought was being treated unfairly. He's not going to change that much."

"He's been through a lot. He's lost a wife and—"

"And you think that's going to make him become corrupt?" Esther asked.

"No. I just…it might make him susceptible to people pretending to be his friend and convincing him to—"

"Emma, that sounds like something out of a dime

novel," Grace, an avid reader, said. "You know he's more sensible than that."

Emma hoped so. Still, she had such a bad feeling about policemen. She'd seen how they treated the people they were supposed to protect and had read too many stories about them being crooked. She just couldn't stand the fact that Sam had become one of them now. But she knew none of that was going to change Grace's and Esther's minds about it all. "I hope he is."

"What we really need to do is pray for his safety," Esther pointed out.

Emma's heart tightened in her chest at the truth in her cousin's words. If he were the kind of policeman he claimed to be, then he could be in danger. There was no way that Commissioner Roosevelt could have gotten rid of all the corrupt cops in his department while he was there—he hadn't had enough time.

"You're right, Esther. We do need to keep him in our prayers," Emma said. For all kinds of reasons.

And she sent up a silent prayer right then and there. *Oh dear Lord, please forgive me for being so rude to Sam. I'm still so disturbed about his decision, even more now that I realize the risks for him either way. Please keep him safe. He is dear to our hearts, and we don't want anything bad to happen to him. Please let him be the kind of man we've always thought him to be. Please keep him from harm. In Jesus' name, I pray, amen.*

Mrs. Holloway came back downstairs and joined them. "I asked Jones to bring us some tea. There are a few details I'd like to go over with you pertaining to the wedding, Esther, if you have time."

"Of course I have time. I can't thank you enough for doing most of this for us. With Andrew's mother in Boston

and both of us working, I don't know how we'd be ready
for a December wedding without your help."

"You probably mean without my taking over," Mrs. Holloway teased. "But I'm glad you don't mind."

"I do have some studying to do," Grace said. "I'll excuse myself, if you don't mind."

"Not at all, dear, we'll just miss your company. But
we don't want your grades to suffer because of us," Mrs.
Holloway said.

"I'll see you in the morning, then," Grace said. But she
turned back just as she reached the door. "Thank you for
inviting Sam to dinner. I think he needs friends right now."

Emma didn't miss the look her little sister shot her. He
did need friends; there was no denying that. He'd lost a
wife, after all. And he didn't have Mrs. Holloway. At least,
he hadn't had her before now. But Emma was sure that now
that she'd met him and knew he was a friend of theirs, she
would always welcome him into her home.

"He seems to be a very nice young man. I'm glad he
found you all. And he is more than welcome here anytime.
I'm sure we'll be seeing more of him."

"Perhaps. If Emma didn't make him want to stay away
by her attitude," Grace said.

"Oh, I think he's man enough to overlook a temporary
lapse in manners," Mrs. Holloway said.

Emma felt even worse. "I'm sorry, Mrs. Holloway. I
truly didn't mean to appear to be rude."

"I know that, dear. You've never been rude to anyone
to my knowledge. And I prefer to put tonight's episode
down to worry about your friend. But I think he'll be able
to handle whatever comes his way. He's already dealt with
a lot in his lifetime. Losing his parents and then his wife."

Mrs. Holloway's words pricked her heart. Sam had been

through a terrible time, and he'd searched them out, and—
there was no denying it—she'd been awful.

Emma felt like crawling into a hole. And she would
have, if one were near.

Sam went to church the next morning feeling a bit unsettled. He'd enjoyed the evening at Mrs. Holloway's a
great deal, but there was no denying that Emma was deeply
unhappy with his decision to become a policeman.

He couldn't really blame her. For most of his life, he'd
detested policemen, too. Had no respect for the ones he
knew and really didn't believe there was a good one in
the lot of them.

But when the opportunity to become one and try to
change the department for the better came to him, he'd
had to do some real soul-searching. Did he want to make
a difference in the city or did he just want to complain?

That's how his father-in-law, William Brisbane, had put
it to him, and Sam was still grateful to the man for his plain
talk and his love. When Sam had had to leave the orphanage, he'd felt adrift and alone, looking for a place to belong.
He'd been working as a delivery boy at the grocery store
William owned, and the man had invited him to church.

Sam went, and Mr. Brisbane's wife had asked him to
come home to Sunday dinner with them. It was there he
fell in love with their daughter, Ann. He'd been going to
church with them ever since.

They'd become the parents Sam needed, stepping in
for those Sam couldn't even remember, and were still a
major part of his life even after Ann's death. They'd all
lost the woman they loved and had a bond that would stay
with them forever.

Now Mr. and Mrs. Brisbane smiled at him as he slid
into the pew and took a seat beside William.

"Good morning, son. We were about to think you weren't going to make it. Thought maybe today was the first day on your new beat."

"No, I start tomorrow," Sam whispered back.

"Good. You can have Sunday dinner with us," Margaret Brisbane leaned forward to say.

Sam nodded just as the service got under way. He loved these two people and knew they were there for him, and always would be. But it wasn't always easy to be around them. Sometimes it brought back too many memories of Ann, and there were times he made excuses and times he was actually glad he could say no because of work. But he didn't want to hurt them, nor the relationship he had with them. So most times he went whenever he was invited. He supposed they all went through the same feelings. Being connected to each other because of Ann and yet saddened to the depth of their hearts that she wasn't there.

But things had become a bit easier once they'd gotten through with all the firsts. The first Thanksgiving and Christmas without her, and seeing the New Year in, were the loneliest holidays he'd ever spent. And then, there was Ann's birthday, their wedding anniversary…and that of her death.

Those had been such painful days. And Sam had decided that he never again wanted to go through that kind of hurt. He never intended to fall in love again. He couldn't bear to lose anyone else he loved.

Now he tried to concentrate on the sermon. It was from Isaiah and about forgetting the former things and not dwelling on the past. As the preacher put it, one should look to the future and not to the past, get on with one's life instead of living in the past.

But Sam didn't want to forget Ann. And maybe that was what was bothering him now. Her face was beginning to dim, and if not for the photograph taken on their wedding day, he was afraid he'd forget what she'd looked like. And he hadn't stopped thinking about Emma since last night. Not that he was attracted to her or anything like that—but that he'd disappointed her.

Whatever it was, somehow he felt disloyal to his wife for spending so much time thinking about another woman. But how could he be? Ann wasn't here anymore.

"Son? Sam? Are you all right?"

Sam was standing but didn't remember doing it. Evidently he'd sung the last song and bowed for the prayer, but he couldn't remember any of it. *Oh dear Lord, please forgive me. For being distracted, for—*

"Sam!" Mr. Brisbane nudged his shoulder.

"Oh, I'm sorry, Will. I'm afraid I was distracted."

"It's all right, son. I get that way, too, sometimes. I'm sure the good Lord will forgive us. Long as we don't make a habit of it and don't forget to ask Him to."

"Yes sir. I hope so."

Mr. Brisbane slapped him on the back. "Let's go. Margaret put a nice roast on early this morning, and I'm sure it's going to make our mouths water soon as we walk in the door."

"I made your favorite pie, too, Sam," Mrs. Brisbane said.

"You did? Cherry?"

"Yes. And I've got some homemade ice cream to go with it."

Besides Mrs. Robertson, this woman was the closest thing to a mother he'd ever had. He couldn't really remember the woman who'd given him birth—and he loved his mother-in-law. He certainly didn't want to put a damper on her day or her effort to please him. "Let's get going, then."

They were midway through one of the best meals Sam

had ever eaten when William cleared his throat. "Sam, Margaret and I...well, we've been talking, and we feel it's time we told you..."

"What is it, William? Is something wrong?"

"Oh no, Sam. It's nothing like that. Just something we want you to know so that you don't ever have to worry about it," Margaret said.

Relief surged through Sam. He loved these two people and never wanted to hurt them.

"We just want you to know that, if you should ever become interested in another woman, want to remarry—"

"Oh, you don't have to worry about that, William. I don't see myself ever remarrying. I can't even..." Sam began to shake his head.

"Son, we aren't worried about it. We just want you to know that should you find someone who can change your mind and you decide to remarry, we'll be happy for you. Ann wouldn't want you to live the rest of your life alone. We know that and deep down, so do you. We'd just love to still be part of your life if that happens, and we'll welcome anyone you fall in love with to this home."

Sam closed his eyes against the sudden sting behind them. "Thank you. I can't imagine it ever happening, but if it ever does, she'll have to accept the two of you as my family. You're the only parents I have."

William nodded. "And you're the only child we have left."

Margaret jumped up from the table. "I'll go get that pie now."

But Sam could tell she was wiping her eyes as she headed for the kitchen. He truly was blessed to be loved by these two people.

Chapter 4

"Operator? Operator, are you there?"

"Yes ma'am, what may I do for you?" Emma recognized the voice on the other end of the line and cringed. Mrs. Alma Vaughn always had a complaint of some kind.

"What took you so long?"

"I'm sorry, I was connecting another line."

"Humph! Well, connect me with the Harry Cannon home, please. I need to speak to Mrs. Cannon."

"Yes ma'am. Right away," Emma said, plugging Mrs. Vaughn's line into that of Mrs. Cannon. She waited only until the connection had been made to turn her attention to the next caller. There were conversations she wouldn't mind listening in on, some she couldn't help but hear, but she went to great lengths not to stay on the line any longer than necessary when it was Mrs. Vaughn. She'd heard tales about her reporting an operator for eavesdropping, and Emma wasn't about to let it happen to her. Not if she could help it.

As always, the day seemed to fly by, and Emma was happy when quitting time came around. Her relief was a young man named Harold, and Emma handed him her headset and quickly vacated the seat so that he could answer an incoming call.

They'd never really talked and only nodded to each other most days. Several other operators left the same time she did but went their separate ways as soon as they left the building. Emma and one other girl, Mary White, caught the same trolley for part of the way home.

"It was really busy today, wasn't it?" Mary asked.

"It was. I had a lot of requests to connect to the Waldorf."

"I believe the Astors are having a ball there this weekend," Mary said.

"Yes, some kind of charity event, I believe. At least I thought I saw something in Sunday's paper about it." Emma usually checked the society page every day. Their callers all seemed to think they should know everything that went on in this city.

"Judging from all the comments I heard today, it's big, and everyone who is someone in this city is expected to show up."

Emma laughed. "That certainly doesn't include us, does it?"

"No, I don't believe it does. But I will certainly be reading Sunday's paper to hear all about it."

"Yes, so will I," Emma said. She was already living a life she never dreamed of having. She truly had no desire to be any wealthier than she felt right now.

Their trolley came to a stop, and Mary got up to catch the next one that would take her home. "I'll see you tomorrow. Have a nice evening."

"You, too, Mary," Emma said.

Another person took Mary's seat on the trolley, and Emma was glad to have the window seat. All day Sunday she'd wondered if Sam would show up again after her rudeness on Saturday. But if he didn't, then surely she'd run into him sooner or later. He did patrol their neighborhood, after all.

She looked out both sides of the trolley as it came closer to her stop, wondering if she might catch a glimpse of him. But she wasn't prepared for it when she actually did see him.

Sam was standing at the trolley stop, talking to some young men. But as the trolley came to a stop, he said a few words to them and then turned just as she stepped off the trolley. His smile reached into the depths of her heart and eased the tightness she'd felt since being so rude to him on Saturday.

"Good afternoon, Emma."

"How are you today, Sam? This is your first day in the neighborhood, isn't it?" He looked tall and handsome in his police uniform.

"It is. I wondered if you might be on this trolley. Since this is part of the area I patrol, I'm trying to get familiar with the people that get on and off at different times of the day."

"Oh." Any thought that he might have only been waiting for her dissipated as quickly as it'd come.

He shrugged and began walking along with her. "It makes it easier to get to know the people who actually live in the neighborhood."

"So, you'll visit each stop?"

"At some point, yes."

"It's not just you patrolling this area, is it?"

Sam chuckled. "Of course not. One man couldn't cover it all. But we all have to get to know the whole area over

time. The men I'm working with already know it pretty
well, and they've been helping me a lot today."

"I hope they—"

"Emma, they're good men. They really are. Things are
going to change. You'll see."

"I hope so. And, Sam?"

"Yes?"

"I'm sorry I wasn't more supportive the other night."

"It's all right, Emma. I understand why you feel the
way you do. I just pray that over time you'll be able to
trust the department."

Emma wasn't sure that would ever happen, but she
would pray that it would.

"Mrs. Holloway said you are welcome anytime, so don't
make a stranger of yourself," Emma said. The best way to
keep an eye on Sam would be to have him around often.

"I won't. I want an invitation to Esther's wedding." He
grinned.

"I'll be sure to tell her."

"It's easy to see that Dr. Radcliff is very much in love
with her."

"Oh, he is. And the same can be said about Esther toward him. They are a good match for each other."

"They seem to be." Sam turned quiet, and Emma wondered if she'd brought up sad memories for him. "I'm happy
for all of you that Mrs. Holloway stepped into your lives."

"Oh, so are we. We do know how fortunate we are and
never want to take her or what she's given us for granted. If
not for her, I'd probably be living at the YWCA and Grace
would still be at the orphanage. Oh, we know she would
have been all right with Mrs. Robertson, but leaving her
would have torn my heart out."

Sam nodded. "I can understand that, and I'm thankful
that you didn't have to."

"Grace is thriving. She loves Mrs. Holloway, and the school she goes to, and has made some new friends. But she still likes to visit her friends at the orphanage, and I think that's a good idea."

"It is, for all kinds of reasons. It will give the others hope that they can have a good life, too. It will let them know that you haven't forgotten them and that you still care about them. And it will keep you all—"

Sam broke off, but Emma thought she knew what he'd been about to say. "Keep us humble? If so, you're right, it will. We promised each other when Mrs. Holloway first took us in that we wouldn't let ourselves get so used to the new lifestyle that we would forget where we came from."

"I really wasn't worried that you would, but I'm glad you are as down to earth as always." Sam grinned. "I did miss you all, and now I wish that I'd been better about visiting the orphanage after I left. I think I might check with Mrs. Robertson and see if there are any boys that need some extra attention and guidance from a man. It would have been nice to have one to turn to when I was there. Oh, we did have men teachers at school, but they didn't really put forth much of an effort with us. I'd like to take at least a day or two a week to spend some time with the boys at the orphanage."

"That is a good idea, Sam. I'm sure most of the boys there would benefit from having you to talk to. I'd never really thought about it, but it must have been very difficult growing up without a man to turn to at times." It had to be more than difficult…there had to be questions a boy would want to ask someone besides a woman. "How—whom did you talk to when you needed to talk to a man?"

Sam shrugged. "We mostly talked to each other and put what little knowledge we had together. And some of the older boys did try to be there for the ones coming up.

But they'd never been out on their own, never had to find a job or make a living yet. And I guess by the time they did, they were too busy to realize we still needed to talk. I can't really blame them. I did the very same thing."

"But you're going to change things now?"

"I am," he said, as if he'd made up his mind. "At least I'll see what Mrs. Robertson thinks about it and go from there."

"I can't imagine her not liking the idea, Sam, especially because you were raised there. You know what those boys are dealing with. You won't have to try to put yourself in their place, because you've been there, and they know it." Emma was excited about his idea; surely Mrs. Robertson would be, too.

They'd arrived at Mrs. Holloway's, and Emma turned to Sam. "Would you like to come in? I know everyone would love to see you."

"I'd like to, but I'm not through with my shift yet. Another time, I will, though."

"All right. I'll tell them you'll be stopping by."

Sam pushed his hat back on his head and smiled. "I'll see you soon, Emma."

Sam never had been the kind to carry a grudge, and for that Emma was grateful. "See you, Sam."

She watched him leave and then hurried up the steps, her heart lighter than it had been in two days.

Sam strutted down the street, feeling better than he had in several days. Emma seemed more herself today than she had on Saturday. Maybe she'd had time to realize that he wasn't going to change and that he truly believed the police department was going to get better. He hoped so.

She seemed almost as excited as he was about him working with the boys at the orphanage. He didn't know why he hadn't thought of it sooner, and he suddenly knew how Mrs. Holloway felt about not bringing the girls to live with her sooner. He couldn't wait to talk to Mrs. Robertson about his idea.

Once he and his partner were relieved of their duties, they caught the same trolley. Richard was married and lived a few blocks away from where Sam lived.

"How do you think you're going to like working in Murray Hill?"

"I think it's going to be a lot quieter than where I've been working, but I think I'll like it." It helped that he knew people in the neighborhood and hoped to be able to see them more often.

"It is quiet for the most part, but not always. Still, after you've been working in the Bowery, you'll probably appreciate the calmer atmosphere."

Sam nodded. "There is that."

"You won't be bored, I assure you. There are always mischief makers in these kinds of neighborhoods, and you'd be surprised how many robberies you'll be called in on." Richard laughed and shook his head. "Everything from furniture and jewelry to pies off windowsills. And then of course in the business section, there are attempted robberies and all kinds of troubles. With us switching with other teams, you get to see a lot of everything, just not quite as much violent crime."

"That will be a relief," Sam said. "I've already seen enough violence to last a lifetime."

"It can still happen here, but nowhere near as often," Richard said. "I think you'll like it as much as I do."

The trolley came to a stop, and Richard stood. "See you tomorrow. Have a good evening."

"See you," Sam said. All in all, his first day on his new beat had gone well, and he looked forward to learning the area and the people. In a few weeks he'd feel more comfortable, he was sure. And it helped that he knew Mrs. Holloway and would be seeing the girls. He'd been pleased to find out what trolley Emma rode to work and back, and he knew he'd manage to see more of her in the days to come. The thought had him looking forward to the rest of the week.

He grabbed a bite to eat at one of the nearby cafés and then headed over to the orphanage to talk to Mrs. Robertson. No need in putting it off. He wanted to speak to her while she could sense his excitement about trying to prepare some of the boys for life on their own.

Although it was a bit later than he would normally visit, Sam hoped she'd be able to talk to him. Usually things were quieting down this time of day.

One of the older boys answered the door, and his face split into a huge grin. "Sam? Sam Tucker? It that you?"

"It is. And you're—"

"Walter Renfro. I was only about twelve when you left."

"I remember you, Walter." He was a good kid, tried to follow the rules and help the younger kids. Maybe he'd be a help with Sam's endeavor if Mrs. Robertson liked the idea. "Do you think you could see if Mrs. Robertson has a few minutes free for me?"

"Sure. Come on in."

Walter hurried off only to return with Mrs. Robertson following right behind.

She seemed as glad to see him as she had a few days earlier. "Sam, how good to see you again so soon! Come in. What brings you here?"

"I have an idea I'd like to present to you if you have a little time."

"Of course I do." She turned to Walter. "Would you

make sure the younger boys are getting ready for bed, Walter?"

"Yes ma'am. It's good to see you, Sam."

"Same to you, Walter. I hope to see you again soon."

"Let's go into my office and talk. Would you like me to have some coffee sent in?"

"No ma'am. I'm fine."

He followed her into her office, and once she'd taken her seat, he took the one across from her.

"Now, what is this idea you have?"

Sam began to explain what it was he wanted to do, and he could tell she was interested by her smile and the way her eyes lit up.

"Oh Sam. I can't begin to tell you how proud I am of you and how excited I am about your idea. Having a man take interest in them, helping them get ready for the time when they must leave and get out on their own is exactly what my boys need. I've tried to get something like this started before, but I haven't garnered the support I wanted. You do realize that it's something that you can't do one day and then just drop? That would be worse than not helping at all. Most of these young people have had more than their share of disappointment in their lifetimes. But of course you know that."

"I do. And that is why I want to do something to help and to try and make it easier for them when they leave here."

"I'm all for it. You plan how you want to do it. I have two young men who will be leaving next year—Walter Renfro and Carl White. They are both good boys, but I think they are a bit nervous about going it alone. Will you be able to work with both of them, or were you thinking one-on-one?"

"I'll work with however many I need to. At first I'd

thought one-on-one, and I can still do some of that. But maybe if I can get together with both of them, I can help them stay in touch with each other after they leave?"

"That would be a great idea. When do you want to start? You know you could come to dinner and then maybe—"

"Visit with them for a while? Get to know them and gain their trust?"

"Yes. Sam, this is going to be such a major help to these boys, I can't tell you how happy I am that you've thought of it. I worry about these young people having to get out on their own without any guidance once they leave here. Your idea is an answer to a prayer."

Her words humbled Sam, and he wondered again why he'd never thought of doing this before now. Probably, like many, he'd been eager to get out on his own, thinking he knew what he was doing, only to find he didn't have any idea how hard it would be or how lonely.

"I'm glad you like my idea. With the Lord's help, I'm sure it will work out."

"I am, too," Mrs. Robertson said. "Now as I said, you figure out what will work best for you and we'll get started. I'm not going to say anything to the boys until you decide best how to get started. But get back to me soon as you can. With them leaving next summer, we can't get started soon enough."

Sam nodded. "For starters, why don't I come to supper tomorrow night and we'll see if the boys are even interested?"

"That sounds great. I'm sure they will be. They were young when you left, but they looked up to you a lot, just as the younger boys now look up to them. Only they don't really realize it."

"I can understand that. I didn't either. I wish I had. But now is the time to remedy some of that." He stood. "I'll let you get everyone settled down and I'll see you tomorrow evening. Supper is still at six?"

"It is. I'll see you out. Sam, I can't tell you how proud I am of you."

"Thank you, Mrs. Robertson. But I'm still a work in progress. I hope not to disappoint you."

"You won't. I'm sure of it. See you tomorrow. I'll make sure we have one of your favorite meals."

Sam headed back to his room feeling as if he might actually be able to make a difference in some of the boys' lives. With the help of the Lord, he was going to do all he could.

If it weren't so late, he'd think about going over to talk to Emma about it right then. She seemed to think it was as good an idea as he did. He'd like to tell her Mrs. Robertson did, too. He wondered if he might get her interested in doing something similar for the girls.

Chapter 5

Emma felt a little disgruntled when she didn't see Sam the next day—or the next. She wasn't sure why she should feel that way. He was working, after all, and he'd never promised to meet her trolley every day.

Part of her problem was that when she'd told everyone she'd run into Sam and that he'd said he'd be coming around, they seemed to expect him to do it right away—as she had. But after several days of not running into him at the trolley and him not coming by, they were back to blaming her for his not showing up. And so was she.

But she couldn't help that it bothered her so much that he'd become a policeman. It just did. Still, she was disappointed that he hadn't come by. It was as if she needed to see him to make sure others weren't corrupting him in some way in the department. And yet—she knew Sam. Surely he couldn't change that much. He could be a policeman one could trust—if one could trust any of them.

Emma sighed with aggravation at herself, and at her family for blaming her because Sam hadn't dropped by. They weren't much happier than she was that he'd become a policeman—they just hid it better.

The trolley stopped at Mary's stop, and even she could tell Emma wasn't in the best of moods when she sat down beside her.

"What happened, Emma? You look like you've lost your best friend."

For some reason, she felt that way, but as she couldn't explain it there was no reason to say so. "Just out of sorts, I guess."

"Maybe you got out of bed on the wrong side?"

"I wish I had that excuse, but no, I got out on the right side, but maybe not with the right attitude." Suddenly, Emma remembered the dream she'd been having right before she woke up. In it, she saw Sam getting beaten up and she didn't know if it was by criminals or other policemen. Suddenly she realized that part of her problem with him being a cop was that she was afraid he would be hurt—or worse.

"Maybe you had a bad dream."

"I did."

"That was it, then. I don't like bad dreams," Mary said. "They always set me on edge."

The memory of the nightmare—for that was what it was—came to Emma in full color, and she shook her head to get it out of her mind. She'd pray not to have any more of those kinds of dreams again. And for the Lord to keep Sam safe from all harm.

"That was probably it. But I'm going to stop thinking about it and try to get in a better mood."

"Good."

They talked about all manner of things—comparing

notes from their newspaper reading so they were up on all the happenings around the city. It still amazed Emma that callers seemed to think they were in on everything that went on, from the social activities of the very rich to what went on in city hall—and everything in between.

But it kept her aware of what went on in her city in a way she never had been before, and she realized more and more each day how blessed she was.

"You were right about the Astors hosting a ball this weekend. I suppose we'd better read the society page from front to back on Sunday so we can find out how it went. Several of my callers who didn't manage to get invited are bound to want to know—even though I'm sure they read the same papers we do."

Mary laughed. "They just want to talk it over as if they were there. I wonder what it would be like to be at one of those things?"

"I don't know, and truthfully, I'm afraid I'd work up such a case of nerves I wouldn't enjoy myself anyway. But it would be nice to see what all the ladies are wearing in color instead of black and white. The photographs just don't do justice to the wonderful descriptions."

"I know."

The trolley stopped on the corner just down from the telephone company, and they got off and hurried to work. Their supervisor frowned on tardiness, so they quickly relieved the night shift.

"It's going to be busy this morning," Harold said. "Those women are already trying to find out what their friends are wearing to the charity ball this weekend. You'll be able to handle it much better than I can," he said as she put on the headset and slipped into the chair just as he slid out of it.

He wasn't kidding her. The board was lit up everywhere,

and Emma quickly got to work connecting first one and then another caller. She glanced down the line and saw Mary and the others doing the very same thing. Looked like the day was going to fly by.

She smiled as a familiar line lit up, and she quickly put the pin in. "Central. What may I do for you today, Mrs. Granville?"

"Why Emma, I'm so glad it's you and not that young man. He is no help at all today," Mrs. Granville said. She was one of the sweetest callers Emma dealt with. But she seemed a bit flustered today.

"What happened?"

"I asked him to connect me to the Waldorf so that I could check on the room I've reserved for Saturday evening. It's just too hard for me to get dressed here and stay so late. I like being where all the action is, you know."

Emma stifled a giggle. Mrs. Granville had mentioned that on her next birthday she'd be turning eighty. Emma was encouraged to see that she was still very active at her age. That meant Mrs. Holloway could be, too, and she wanted her to be around as long as possible.

"Didn't he do that?"

"No. He said the line was busy and to try later."

"I'm sorry, Mrs. Granville. We have had a lot of calls for them lately, but let me try. It might take a few minutes though, so please be patient."

Emma breathed a sigh of relief when she was able to connect Mrs. Granville immediately. Sweet as she was, one never knew when a caller would request to speak to a supervisor.

By the end of her shift she'd heard snippets of conversations about the upcoming charity ball—from what dressmaker one family was using to where they'd found the perfect shoes to go with their outfit. Emma couldn't help but wonder if they ever wore the same dress to a different ball, or did they have a new one made for each one?

She and Mary headed home comparing notes on what they knew. It wasn't much when it only came in snippets before another line lit up. It was hard not to listen in for a second or two, and they'd even caught their supervisor doing the same thing.

"You really never long to go to one of these functions?" Mary asked.

Emma laughed. "I can't imagine it. Not something on that scale."

"I can't either. And I'd be so nervous about it I wouldn't be able to have a good time, anyway."

"I feel the same way," Emma said. "But I do like hearing about it and imagining what it would be like."

"Yes, so do I," Mary agreed. The trolley pulled up at Mary's stop and she stood and shook her skirts before leaving. "See you tomorrow, Emma."

"See you, then."

For the rest of the ride to her trolley stop, Emma gazed out the window, wondering if Sam might be at her stop to meet her when she got there, and her pulse gave a little jump when she saw him standing at the corner. He was there. She couldn't stifle her smile as she stood and shook out her skirts before stepping out of the trolley.

Emma's smile made Sam glad he'd made the effort to be there when she got home from work.

"Sam. I'd begun to think you'd been transferred to another beat."

"No. Just been working at the other end of this one. I'm glad to be back today. I was hoping to catch you."

"You don't need to catch me. You can stop by anytime."

"I was going to do that if you hadn't been here. I've

been wanting to tell you that I spoke with Mrs. Robertson and she really likes my idea about helping the young men at the orphanage."

They fell in step together, and Emma smiled up at him. "I told you she would."

"You did. I do have another idea I'd like to run by you though."

"Oh? What is that?"

"I know the girls have Mrs. Robertson to turn to. But I began to think that, well, you know, some of them won't talk to her about everything—it might be easier for them to talk to someone nearer their age. And for those about to leave, they are no different than the boys. They need to talk to someone who has left and is working now. I thought you might be interested in working with them."

"Oh, I'd love it, Sam, but I know how fortunate we are to be living with Mrs. Holloway. Not all the girls are going to be so—"

"No, they won't. But you are still working, are you not?"

"Yes…"

"And they are going to have to work, too. I'm sure you can give them good advice about how to find a job and keep it."

"I believe I could do that. I'd like to help; you know that."

"I do. That's why I wanted to tell you about it. I haven't said anything to Mrs. Robertson about it, but I'm sure she'll love the idea."

"I think she'd be happy with anything we can do to help the others."

"I thought Esther and Grace might want to help, too. Grace has awhile before she starts working, but just visiting the younger girls and being a friend to them will prepare her to help when the time comes for them to leave."

"That is a very good idea, Sam. Why don't you come in and explain it all to them—or are you still on duty?"

"I am. But if you think it might be all right with Mrs. Holloway, I could come by later."

"I'm sure it will be fine with her. In fact, why don't you come for supper? I know she'd be happy to set another place. She always has more than enough food."

"Are you sure I won't be imposing?"

"I'm certain you won't. In fact, you'd help me out if you'd come."

"How so?"

"The girls believe you haven't come back because I was so rude to you the other day and—"

"Say no more. What time?"

"Around six thirty. We'll eat at seven."

"I'll be there."

"Good. I'll see you then," Emma said before running up the steps to Mrs. Holloway's home.

Sam turned away, a spring in his step and a smile on his face. He was glad he'd been assigned to this beat and very happy that he'd connected with Emma, Grace, and Esther once more. He looked forward to talking to them about helping at the orphanage, but he really didn't think it would take much convincing. They were keeping in contact with their friends there already. Something he should have done and hadn't. But he intended to make up for his neglect now.

Emma was pleased that she'd finally seemed to redeem herself in Grace's and Esther's eyes for her bad behavior toward Sam.

"He's really coming for supper?" Grace asked.

"He really is. He has something he wants to talk to us about pertaining to the orphanage."

"Oh?" Esther asked. "What is it?"

"I'll let him explain it all." She looked over at Mrs. Holloway who was pouring her a cup of tea. "You don't mind him coming this evening, do you, Mrs. Holloway?"

"You know I don't, dear. He's a friend to all of you, and I look forward to getting to know him better." She handed Emma her cup.

"How is it you're the only one running into him?" Esther asked as Emma took a seat beside Grace.

"Both times I've seen him at the trolley stop, so I suppose he's patrolling in our area on those days."

"Probably."

"He's very handsome, isn't he?" Grace asked.

"Grace, are you sweet on Sam?" Emma teased.

"Oh my goodness, no. He's much too old for me. And Esther is spoken for. But you aren't. He'd make a fine husband, I'd think."

"Oh Grace! I'm not looking for a husband at present, although I would like to marry one day. Besides, Sam is probably still grieving the death of his wife. And furthermore, I don't like him being a cop, as you well know."

Grace shrugged. "It was just a thought. I'm happy that he's still our friend."

"Yes, so am I," Esther said. "Don't worry, Emma, we won't try to matchmake."

"I would certainly hope not."

"Emma doesn't need anyone to matchmake for her besides the Lord," Mrs. Holloway said. "He'll bring the right person into her life when the time is best."

Emma sighed, appreciative for the intervention. "Thank you, Mrs. Holloway." It wasn't that Sam wasn't someone she could be interested in. It was that she didn't want to lose her heart to him. His job was too dangerous in too many ways; and besides, she truly didn't want to come in second to his deceased wife. She wanted to be the love of her husband's life—not the one he settled for after losing her.

Still, once she went up to change for dinner, she dressed with care. She at least wanted Sam to think of her as a woman now and not the young adolescent he'd known at the orphanage.

She chose a blue-and-green-striped dress that brought out the green flecks in her eyes, and she took extra time with her hair, putting it up in a neat chignon she'd just recently learned to do. She pinched her cheeks to give them more color and brushed her eyebrows to form a neat arch. She bit her lips lightly to give them some color and finally decided she'd have to do.

"You look very nice, Emma," Esther said, coming out of her room at the same time. "Mrs. Holloway is right. You don't need us to matchmake for you. I'm sure you'll have several potential beaus calling before very long."

"You know, I've mentioned that I want to get married instead of going off to school and having a career like you do—of course, you're managing to do both—but I do like my job as a telephone operator, and I'm not in a huge hurry to marry," Emma said as they headed down the staircase. "I know I don't want to marry just for the sake of being married. I want true love like you and Andrew have."

"I know you do. And you'll have it, of that I'm sure. Just don't settle for anything else."

"I don't intend to. But right now, I'm just anxious for you and Grace to hear what Sam has to say. He's got some great ideas about helping at the orphanage."

"I'm looking forward to hearing them," Esther said as they entered the parlor where Andrew and his aunt awaited them.

"What is it you want to hear, my love?" Andrew asked

as he crossed the room to place a light kiss on Esther's cheek.

Emma smiled at the way Esther always blushed when he kissed her in front of family. Oh yes, she wanted a love like theirs, and she'd wait however long it took to find it.

"Sam is coming to talk to us about some ideas he has for the orphanage. Did Mrs. Holloway tell you?"

"I only had time to tell him that Mr. Tucker was coming for dinner before you came in, dear," Mrs. Holloway explained.

"I'm curious to hear what he has to say," said Andrew. "I must admit that I have a soft spot for the orphanage since the first time I visited there with all of you. Mrs. Robertson is doing a fine job, but it can't be easy, and I'm sure she could use help in all kinds of ways."

Jones appeared at the door. "Mr. Tucker is here, Mrs. Holloway."

"Please show him in, Jones," Mrs. Holloway said.

Sam entered dressed in a nice suit, something Emma had never seen him in. He looked quite distinguished all dressed up, although she thought she liked him in his uniform even more—much as she wished it were one other than a policeman's.

"Good evening, Mr. Tucker," Mrs. Holloway said.

"Good evening, Mrs. Holloway, Dr. Radcliff, and—"

Grace giggled. "Good evening, Sam. You don't have to say all our names, but it's good to know you have those kinds of manners."

"Unlike you, Grace. You seem to have forgotten yours. You should have let him finish," Esther teased with a twinkle in her eyes. "I'm afraid she's gotten lax with her manners, Sam. But it is good to see you."

Mrs. Holloway laughed. "Now you see why I enjoy

these girls so. They've taken the stuffiness right out of this house."

"Dinner is ready whenever you are, ma'am," Jones said.

"We're ready. I'm glad you've joined us tonight, Mr. Tucker," Mrs. Holloway said.

"Please, ma'am. Call me Sam. May I escort you to the dining room?"

"Please do, Sam." She smiled and took the arm he proffered.

Chapter 6

Sam seated Mrs. Holloway, and then himself at the seat she'd pointed out was his, which happened to be right next to Emma's. He didn't think he'd ever eaten in a dining room as nice as this one. At first he felt a little out of place, and then he realized that his old friends had adjusted to living here—surely he could get through a meal without totally embarrassing himself.

"Sam, Emma tells us you have some plans pertaining to the orphanage you'd like to talk about. I'm eager to hear them," Andrew said once they'd been served and he'd said the blessing.

"I do. I'm going to be helping with some of the young men who'll be leaving before too long. Mrs. Robertson and I thought that it would be good for someone who was raised there and has gotten out on his own and started working to help prepare them for their new lives."

"That's a really good idea, Sam. It must be very difficult to start a new life when you don't really know what to expect," Andrew said.

"That's it exactly. And it's equally hard for both boys and girls. That's why I thought Emma, Esther, and Grace might want to try to help, too."

"I'm not old enough to help in that way," Grace said.

"Oh, but if you keep your friendships intact as you are trying to do," Sam said, "you will be a huge help to the girls you're friends with when it's time for them to leave."

"I suppose."

"And Emma is out working now. She knows what it's like to be an employee and what is expected of her. The girls about to get out on their own don't know any of that."

"That's true," Emma said.

"And Esther is living her dream. They need to see that their dreams can come true, too."

Esther nodded. "I think you've come up with a wonderful idea, Sam. We have tried to keep in touch, but we need to do more."

"There might be other ways we could help," Andrew said. "I'd like to offer my services for free when one of the orphans gets sick. I'm sure Mrs. Robertson has other physicians she can call, but I'd like to be added to the list."

"I'm sure she'd be glad to have another doctor to call on," Sam said. "I'm also hoping to help some of those kids learn to trust me—even when I'm in uniform."

"Looked at you a little warily, did they?"

"No. They haven't seen me in uniform yet. And I only saw Walter the night I went to talk to Mrs. Robertson, and he recognized me. Then when I went to supper to talk to them about it, I wasn't in uniform that time. I'm hoping that by the time they do see me dressed for work, it won't matter."

"What did they think of the plan?" Mrs. Holloway asked.

"They're very excited about it. We haven't said anything to the girls yet because Mrs. Robertson asked me to run it by all of you first and see if it is something you'd like to help with. As she told me—we can't just start it and disappear. It has to be something we're willing to commit to. At least with this group of young people."

"Oh, of course we'd have to keep it up," Emma said. "Quitting would be worse than not doing anything at all."

"Looks like we have some planning to do, then," Sam said.

"Please feel free to use my home at any time for your planning meetings," Mrs. Holloway said. "It could be that I could come up with a few ideas, too."

"I'm certain you could, Aunt Miriam," Andrew said.

"Could we begin tonight so that I can let Mrs. Robertson know what our plans are?" Sam asked.

"I don't know why not," Mrs. Holloway said.

"Let's start right after dinner," Emma suggested.

Sam grinned. He'd prayed they'd come through for him, and they had. He sent up a silent prayer of thanksgiving for those answered prayers.

Over the next few hours they decided that it might be better to have their planning meetings at the same time once every two weeks, but they'd meet separately with the older children at the orphanage.

Then once a month they'd all try to go on an outing together so that both young men and young women would get to know each other a little better and want to stay in contact—especially during that first year on their own.

"I think it is a great plan," Emma said. "I don't know many who have kept in touch, and that is a shame. Esther,

Grace, and I have been blessed to be able to stay together from the beginning. At least we've always had each other."

"If we can help some of them remain friends and be there for each other, we will accomplish a lot." Esther said.

"And you never know. Some of them might end up getting married," Grace said.

"She's been in a matchmaking mood lately. She must be reading too many romantic novels," Esther said with a smile.

"Well, they might," Grace insisted.

"It's actually a good idea, Grace. If not that they might marry, but for the fact that they will have a circle of friends they can turn to," Sam said.

"Thank you, Sam." Grace gave a "so there" kind of grin at Esther, eliciting laughter around the table.

"I think the whole idea is a good one," Mrs. Holloway said. "I'm sure that Mrs. Robertson will be very happy with it."

"I hope so," Sam said. "Mostly, I hope it truly will help those young people about to be responsible for themselves very soon."

"You know, if any of the girls shows an aptitude for office skills, I could use a receptionist," Andrew said.

"Oh Andrew, that is a wonderful idea. Your patient list is getting longer all the time and it would free your nurse up if you had someone to take care of the office," Esther said.

"We'll find out."

"I wouldn't mind having that job. But I suppose I need to finish school first," Grace said.

"Yes ma'am, you do," Emma said to her little sister.

"I'm sure we'll find you something you love to do by then, Grace. I thought you might want to be a librarian," Andrew suggested.

Grace caught her breath and let it out slowly. "You know that would be the perfect career for me. Books everywhere. I can't think of anything I'd like more."

"Unless it would be to *write* your own book," Emma said.

"Ooh. Do you think I could?"

"If I can become a pharmacist, you could certainly become an author," Esther said.

"I think I might just do that."

"And I think you should," Emma said.

Sam loved the way the three girls interacted with each other. He wished he'd had a sibling or any kind of family at all.

"I think it's all going to work out fine. But I'm glad that you'll all get together at least several times a month to talk to each other about how things are going," Mrs. Holloway said. "Sam, you are welcome here for dinner any night you'd like, but in addition to that, why don't you all plan on being here on your meeting nights, and after dinner you can discuss how the meetings with your young people went and what might need to be done next."

"Why, thank you, Mrs. Holloway. I appreciate that. It does get tiresome eating alone. And I appreciate being able to meet here." He liked that idea very much. Not only would it be good for planning—it would give him someplace to be, people he cared about to be with.

He knew he'd been lonely, but he didn't realize quite how much until he'd reconnected with Esther and her cousins.

"I think that is a very good idea, Aunt Miriam," Andrew said. "What night would work for all of you?"

"Actually, since Mrs. Holloway is offering the use of her home, we should let her decide," Emma said.

Mrs. Holloway thought for a moment. "Well, Sam, I

know that you do change shifts some—what would work best for you?"

"I do change shifts every other week. I'm on days this week, so I will be on nights the next, but right now my day off is on Sunday. I'm hoping to keep it that way so that I can attend church."

"All right then, why don't we have a Sunday night supper?"

"Would that work for everyone?"

"It should," Andrew said. "I might be called out on an emergency, but otherwise I can't see why it wouldn't work for me. What about the rest of you?"

"Thankfully I'm not working nights, so it will work for me," Emma said.

"Me, too," Esther added.

"We all know any night will work for me," Grace said. "I like the idea of a Sunday night supper though."

"So do I. Perhaps I could ask Mr. Collins to join us?" Mrs. Holloway suggested.

"Mr. Collins?" Sam asked.

"He owns Collins Pharmacy. I'm doing my apprenticeship under him," Esther said.

"And he's a special friend of Mrs. Holloway's," Grace said. "We all like him very much."

"I think Mrs. Holloway should be able to ask anyone she wishes to," Sam said.

"Good, then, would you like to start this Sunday?"

Everyone agreed to begin as soon as possible.

"I'll speak to Mrs. Robertson and let her know everyone is on board with helping," Sam said.

"You may invite her on Sunday, too, if she's available, Sam," Mrs. Holloway offered.

"I'll let her know."

By the time Sam left that evening, Emma was excited

about the plans they'd made to help the other orphans. She walked him to the door.

"Thank you for asking me to dinner, Emma. I'm so glad everyone liked my ideas."

"I am, too. It will feel good to be doing something to help other orphans. And we know what it is they need to know."

Sam nodded. "Mostly they need to know someone cares enough to make things easier for them."

Emma nodded. "And the three of us are so fortunate that Mrs. Holloway came along. I hope the others don't resent us because we haven't had to be totally on our own."

"They might not have a Mrs. Holloway in their lives, Emma, but neither are they going to be totally on their own. Not with our support. Oh, they may not have a fine home to live in, but they will have us to turn to."

Emma nodded. She hoped the young people would accept the friendship they'd offer and realize that she and Grace and Esther truly wanted to help them. She followed Sam out the door.

He turned to her. "I suppose I'll see you Sunday night, if not before?"

"Yes. I think Mrs. Holloway is almost as excited about it as we are," Emma said.

"Good, she deserves to be part of it, too. If anyone knows how to make a difference in the life of an orphan, she does."

Emma smiled. "That is so true, she does. I'm glad we're going to be meeting at the house."

"So am I. But part of my reasoning is selfish. I'm glad to be in contact with you and Grace and Esther again. It's been a tough year, and now that we have a plan to help others, I'm beginning to feel as if I can look forward to the future again."

Emma's heart twisted at his words. How awful it must be to have lost a mate. To dread the future without that person one loved. "I'm sorry it's been so hard for you, Sam. I'm glad you've found something that is helping you go forward."

He nodded. "So am I. Thank you for agreeing to help with my plan."

"You're welcome. Thank you for asking us to."

Sam smiled at her and gave a little salute before descending the steps to the street. "Good night, Emma."

"Good night, Sam."

Chapter 7

Waiting for her trolley the next morning, Emma found herself looking forward to the coming Sunday night supper. She loved Sam's idea of helping at the orphanage. And she'd enjoyed having him at supper the night before.

She still didn't like that he was a policeman—she didn't think it was possible that she ever would. And she still worried that he might in some way be influenced by the corruption she knew still existed in the department. One couldn't get rid of all the bad that had built up over the decades in only a few years. All she knew to do about it was to pray for Sam to stay the kind of man who wanted to reach out to help others and to ask the Lord to help her tamp down the doubts about him that sometimes surfaced. Was it possible that he was only doing these good things to cover up something else?

She hated those thoughts when they came to her and prayed for them to go away. Sam had always been a good person—at least she believed him to be—and she wanted to continue to believe in him. Wanted to believe his desire to help the orphanage and to make a difference in the police force was real.

It made her want to make a difference in the lives of those she knew and cared about at the orphanage, too. After all, she hadn't been away all that long, and she didn't want any of the children there to feel she'd deserted them.

As much as she loved her life at Mrs. Holloway's, she almost felt guilty for how good it was. Most of those leaving the orphanage didn't have it nearly as good. Thankfully there were rooms at the YWCA and the YMCA, but that wasn't the same as a home with people who truly cared about you.

Her work situation would be the same as they would experience though, and she could help there. And she knew in her heart that Mrs. Holloway would welcome any of their friends into her home once in a while. She'd invited them to her birthday party, after all.

The trolley came to a stop, and she quickly stepped on. She even looked forward to work today. She'd managed to read the society page this morning in preparation for the questions she'd be asked—even knowing she wouldn't have all the answers some of the callers would seek.

Tomorrow would be even busier, with everyone wanting an accounting of who was there and what they wore. It was her Sunday to work, and as much as she hated missing church, at least the day would pass fast with all the calls that would be placed to rehash the ball or find out what people could, if they weren't invited.

The trolley stopped at Mary's corner, and she quickly took the seat open next to Emma. "Are you ready for today?"

"I think so. It will be exciting, anyway."

They talked about the articles they'd read, comparing notes, and by the time they arrived at the telephone office they felt as prepared as possible for the busy day ahead.

Harold lost no time in trading places with her. "I am so glad to see you. These women are driving me crazy wanting more information about the ball, the guest list, and the gossip. It's been all I could do to be civil to them. I'm a man! I don't really care about the ball."

"At least you'll have a quiet night."

"I hope so."

Emma couldn't help but giggle as he hurried away.

But lines were lighting up over her board and she quickly got to work. One didn't have to listen in on conversations—the callers wanted a chat with the operators before they ever asked to be connected. Once or twice, Emma had calls that only wanted to find out what she knew. Then when she asked whom she could connect them to, they said no one. It seemed they were getting all the information they needed from her.

That unsettled her. Was *she* keeping the conversation going? Or were *they*? She certainly didn't want to lose her job. For the next few callers, she tried to ask whom they wanted to be connected to before they could launch into any questions.

But it didn't work with Mrs. Fields. She continued to ask questions until Emma finally had to say, "My board is lighting up, and ma'am, I have to go. Whom can I connect you to?"

Only then did the woman tell her whom she wanted to talk to. Her supervisor came by about the time Emma let out a huge sigh and connected the two lines.

"Are you having a problem, Miss Chapman?"

"No ma'am. Well, yes. It's very hard to not have a conversation with our callers today."

"Oh yes, I know. I've been relieving the line. We do realize that sometimes our callers just want to talk to someone who might have more information than they do. As long as it doesn't keep you from connecting others, don't worry about it. I've been in your seat before and I know what you deal with. We aren't going to fire someone who is trying to do their job in spite of constant interruptions."

"Oh, that is a relief, ma'am."

"I believe it's time for your lunch. Go on and enjoy a few moments of peace."

"Thank you, I will." They quickly switched places, and Emma didn't tarry, heading for the lunchroom as fast as her feet would take her.

Sam was beginning to like his new beat a lot. For the most part it was so much calmer than his last one, he almost felt he was getting paid too much.

But Richard assured him that wasn't the case. "We have a larger area to cover, Sam. And I for one am thankful we don't have as much crime as the Bowery does. Still, we have enough to keep us on the lookout."

The business side of his beat was something altogether different from the Bowery; still, it had areas to watch for. He'd been making the rounds of the businesses and getting to know the owners and employers.

Just this morning, he'd met Mr. Collins and seen Esther at work. She'd been glad to introduce the two men.

"I've already heard about you, Officer Tucker," Mr. Collins had said. "Mrs. Holloway has spoken highly of you, as has Esther."

Sam's heart had warmed at the support he had from the two women. He'd smiled at Esther as she went back to work. "I hope never to disappoint them, sir."

"With that attitude, I'm sure you won't. I'm glad to see

the police department going through changes. I didn't trust the last cop on this beat enough to even tell him of my suspicions. It will be good to have one around I can trust."

"Thank you, sir. Have you been having any troubles lately?"

"Not really. Just a few customers I've been watching. They seem to be watching what goes on up here a little too closely for my comfort."

"You think they might be after medicine they shouldn't have?"

"Possibly. You know many people do get addicted to laudanum and that kind of drug."

"Oh yes, sir, that's why I asked. I ran into that at the Bowery."

"Your last beat was there?"

"Yes sir."

"Then I have no trouble trusting that you can handle this one. I'm sure you deserved a break."

Sam chuckled. "It kept me and my partner busy, that's for sure."

"Well, I'm glad to meet you," Mr. Collins said. "I believe I'll be seeing you again on Sunday night at Mrs. Holloway's?"

"Yes sir, you will."

The older man nodded. "Esther and Miriam have been telling me about your plan to help the orphanage you and the girls were raised in. I'm impressed with it."

"Thank you. It seems the least we can do—to help others coming out behind us."

"Yes. The world would be a much better place if we all thought that way."

"Yes sir, I agree. I suppose I'd better be going now. I've several other businesses to visit before lunch. If you have any suspicions of any wrongdoing, be sure to let me know."

"I will. You have a good day, Officer Tucker."

Sam had given a wave to Esther and strode back out on the street and into the next business—a haberdashery. The owner, a Mr. Morgan, was very nice and carried a wide selection of men's clothing at a fairly decent price. Sam thought he'd be back soon as a customer. If he were going to be invited to dinner at Mrs. Holloway's from time to time, he needed a few new things. He didn't want the girls to be embarrassed for his sake.

"No real problems with theft here?" Sam asked.

"Oh, once in a while someone gets out of here with a belt or a cravat. But nothing big—at least not so far. I've only been at this location for a couple of years. But it seems to be a decent neighborhood," Mr. Morgan said.

Sam nodded. "We want to keep it that way, so you let me know if you see anything suspicious going on. We'll be coming around."

Then he and his partner had met up at lunch and switched ends of the beat. He'd take the residential side of it and Richard would take over the business side. They did the switch most days, and it kept the days from becoming monotonous; plus they hoped to get the people they were to protect to trust both of them.

But he'd found that there were pockets of criminal activity he needed to watch out for, and adolescent boys who had too much free time on their hands. They'd already pulled some pranks he'd had to talk to them about, and he prayed it wouldn't escalate to anything more.

There'd also been a couple of people he was on the watch for. They seemed to be casing out the neighborhood and didn't really belong there. He'd never seen them enter a house in the neighborhood, but he'd seen them more often than he was comfortable with.

"Hey Officer Tucker!" One of the younger boys he'd come to know waved to him from the end of the street.

"Good afternoon, Billy. How are you today?"

"Good. I made an A on my spelling test and Mother is going to be so pleased. Maybe she'll make a chocolate cake for me."

Billy and his family lived two streets over from Mrs. Holloway, and he seemed to be a good kid. He didn't much seem to mind when the other boys teased him about his good grades—just shrugged it off and went on about his business.

Sam was pretty sure that was because of his upbringing. He had parents who were teaching him right. And as far as he could see, after so short a time of patrolling this area, that was the case most of the time in this neighborhood.

But there were those who were spoiled beyond what he'd ever seen, thinking everything was due them. Those were the ones he'd certainly be watching—just as he watched the two Everett boys try to steal a pie off Mrs. Moore's windowsill.

He snuck up behind them, and just as the older one reached out to pick it up, Sam grabbed them both by the collars.

"You little scalawags! You know stealing could land you in jail?"

The younger of the two started to cry. "Please don't put us in jail, Officer Tucker!"

"And why shouldn't I?"

"We're sorry, Officer Tucker. It's just that Mrs. Moore's pies are the best in the neighborhood and—"

"Officer! Boys! What's going on here?" Mrs. Moore asked, looking out her kitchen window.

"These boys have been up to a little mischief, Mrs.

Moore. They seem to like your pies a lot. From the smell of this one, I can see why."

"Phillip and Jack! Why, your mother would be plumb ashamed of you two. If you want one of my pies, all you have to do is ask. I'll be glad to make you one."

"Oh, we know, Mrs. Moore," the older one said.

Sam thought Richard had told him the older one was Phillip and the younger one Jack.

"Come on in and I'll give you a piece of that pie. You, too, Officer Tucker."

"Oh, I can't, ma'am. I'm on duty. And besides, how are we going to teach these boys not to steal if you reward them?"

"Oh, I'm not going to reward them. I'm just filling them up so they can do some chores for me. Their mother has already told me to let her know if they try to pull anything over on me."

"Oh Mrs. Moore. Please don't tell Mama!" Jack pleaded.

"Depends on how well you do the chores I give you. Come on, now. You, too, Officer. I don't want them to eat and try to run. You need to be here to make sure they don't."

"Put that way, how can I refuse?"

Sam thoroughly enjoyed his pie, but he had a feeling those boys were having trouble just getting their pieces down—especially with him watching every bite they took.

Mrs. Moore was one smart woman.

Emma had never been quite so glad for quitting time to get there as she was that day. She was ready for this charity ball to be over with. Oh, there'd been other charity functions and there would be more, but one thrown by one of the wealthiest families in the city was unlike any others.

First there was curiosity over the guest list—and how

many would be invited. Then the questions changed to fashion and trying to get a hint of who was wearing what and which designers they'd used.

Why any of the callers thought their telephone operators knew that kind of thing was beyond Emma, but some of them actually seemed to.

She and Mary both sighed with relief when they took their seats on the trolley; then they looked at each other and began to laugh.

"You know it's a good thing we weren't invited to the ball, because I'm just hoping I have enough energy to make it home," Mary said.

"I feel the same way. I've never had so many lines light up at one time since I began working."

"I'd like to say you'll get used to it, but I'm not sure we can. We only have one headset and two hands."

"True," Emma said. "At least the day went by fast; but still, I feel as if I've been running some kind of race."

"I do wonder what it would be like to go to one of these things," Mary said. "I'd love to go one day. But the dressiest thing I have in my closet is my Sunday dress. I love it and think it's beautiful, but I just wonder what it would feel like to have a dress made only for me by a designer."

"I wonder how much it would cost."

"More than we'll make in several months, I'm sure," Mary said.

"We can dream, I suppose," Emma said. "But most of my dreams aren't about going to charity balls. I'm not sure I'd want to have to worry about showing up in a similar gown as someone else, or to try to keep up with the styles that seem ever changing."

"No, I really wouldn't either. Too much to worry about if one is rich. I'll not pine too much for that kind of life."

Mary laughed. "Besides, I don't really think I have much choice."

"I don't think either of us do."

"Oh, I don't know about you, Emma. You do live in a very nice neighborhood, you know. You might meet someone."

"I'm very fortunate that Mrs. Holloway took me in when it was time for me to leave the orphanage," Emma said.

"Your cousin is engaged to a doctor. It could happen to you."

"And it could happen to you, too, Mary. Your neighborhood is a nice one, too."

Mary shrugged. "It's not too bad. But we're not a wealthy neighborhood to be sure."

"But it's not a poor one either." Emma knew that Mary's father owned a shoe store. He might not be rich, but he did provide a good living.

"True. And I'm content with who I am and where I live. Just once in a while I dream about what it would be like to marry someone rich and handsome."

Emma chuckled. "I don't think I'll hold my breath waiting for someone like that."

"No, I don't suppose I will either," Mary said. The next stop was Mary's and when she got off the trolley, Emma really looked at the neighborhood. The homes weren't as large as Mrs. Holloway's, nor were they quite as nice, but they appeared to be well taken care of and they were separated a bit.

In only a few minutes she was at her stop, and she was more than ready to get home. She was blessed to be living in this neighborhood; there was no doubt about it. At one time some of the very wealthy had lived here, Mrs. Holloway had said, but as they wanted larger and larger homes, they'd moved farther north.

And most of the people here were wealthy by Emma's standards, but nowhere near as wealthy as those attending the ball tonight.

She couldn't help but look for Sam when she started home, but he was nowhere to be seen. She consoled herself by remembering that he'd be at Mrs. Holloway's Sunday night supper. Emma thought she'd come up with a wonderful idea. It would be great to have a planning session on Sundays, and she was glad Mrs. Holloway had asked Sam. He had to be lonely at times, and Emma wondered what it was he did after work.

Did he have other friends he visited besides them? Were they policemen, too? Did they have families? If so, it might be hard for him to be around them.

And he wouldn't just hang out at the orphanage. Maybe his wife had family he was still close to. She hoped so. The thought of him being alone saddened her a great deal.

She was glad he'd come up with a plan for helping at the orphanage. It would give him somewhere to go when he was off duty and a reason to feel needed. And now that he'd enlisted more help, he'd be visiting them more often, too. Hopefully, all of it together would keep him the good man she knew him to be. She prayed so.

Chapter 8

Sam had been looking forward to Sunday night supper all day. He'd gone to church with the Brisbanes and told them about his plan to help at the orphanage, and they were very pleased that he'd gotten more people on board with it.

Then on the way home he'd stopped by the orphanage and filled Mrs. Robertson in on what he and the girls had talked about, inviting her to the Sunday night supper, too.

"I'd love to come once in a while, but I won't be able to make it every time. But, please thank Mrs. Holloway for me and let me know what you all come up with. I can expect to see some of you each Saturday, is that right?"

"Yes ma'am." Sam had been thinking about that, but he wanted to talk his idea over with the others before he said anything to Mrs. Robertson about it.

"If you need to discuss anything with me tonight, feel free to telephone me. I'll be here."

Sam agreed to do just that and then spent the rest of

the afternoon making notes on what he hoped the others might want to do.

By the time he got to the Holloway house he was hungry and happy.

Jones opened the door to him before he ever had a chance to ring the bell. It was obvious that the man took his job as seriously as Sam or Andrew took theirs. He was a man of few words, but there was a kindness that radiated from him and Sam had come to look forward to seeing him.

"Come this way, Mr. Tucker. Everyone is in the parlor."

"I hope I'm not late."

"No sir. We're waiting on Mr. Collins to get here, and he's not late yet. I'm not sure all the girls are down yet either."

"I hope that doesn't mean I'm too early."

"Not at all, sir. Besides, Mr. Andrew is running a bit late tonight. He was called out earlier."

"Oh, I hope his patient is all right."

"Yes sir, so do we. Mr. Tucker," Jones announced once they reached the parlor.

"Good evening, Sam," Mrs. Holloway said. "It's good to see you. I trust you had a pleasant day?"

"I did. I went to church and had Sunday dinner with Ann's parents and had a relaxing afternoon. Then I dropped by and talked to Mrs. Robertson for a bit. And I looked forward to coming here all day, so that made it even better."

"Why, thank you, Sam. We've all looked forward to seeing you again."

Grace hurried into the room, followed by her sister and cousin.

"Sam, I'm sorry we weren't down before you got here,"

Emma said. She looked quite lovely tonight in a summery pink-and-green floral dress.

"We dillydallied the afternoon away and were late changing," Grace informed him.

"You all look quite nice, so it was worth the wait," Sam said.

"Oh, you always say the nicest things, doesn't he, Emma?" Grace said. "If I were a little older—"

"Grace Chapman!" Emma said, shaking her head.

Grace laughed. "Oh, he knows I'm teasing, Emma. Don't you, Sam?"

"I do. And I'm sure that I seem quite old to Grace. Probably even to you, Emma. But if I were a little younger…"

Everyone chuckled at his comeback, and as Sam watched Emma blush a delicate shade of pink, he felt his own neck grow warm. Now why had he said that? He'd made up his mind not to let himself become overly attracted to another woman, and he was determined to follow through with his decision. He never wanted to lose another woman he loved, and the only way to avoid that was to not fall in love.

But still, he was glad to be friends with Emma. It brightened his day to run into her at the trolley stop, to look forward to seeing her…and the others, too, of course.

Thankfully, Emma hadn't seemed any more inclined to show an interest in him, for he wasn't sure what his reaction would be if she had. He thought that she might be as determined not to become interested in him as he was not to become interested in any woman. And he felt that was as much because of his profession as it was him, but he didn't know. He did know that he wanted to prove to her that not all policemen on the force were corrupt and that most wanted to bring honor to their jobs. Hopefully, one day, he would.

"Mr. Collins," Jones announced from the doorway. "And Mr. Andrew has arrived and gone up to change. He said to tell you he'll be down momentarily."

"Thank you, Jones," Mrs. Holloway said. "John, it is good to see you. I'm so glad you could make it."

The older man headed straight toward her, grasped her hands, and kissed her on the cheek. From the expression in their eyes, Sam wondered if there was more than just friendship between the two.

"Thank you for inviting me, Miriam. It's always a pleasure to come to your home and visit with all of you."

Only then did the man turn to greet Esther, Emma, and Grace. "You all look quite lovely tonight."

"Thank you, Mr. Collins," Esther said, followed by Emma and Grace.

Then Mr. Collins turned to Sam and smiled. "Officer Tucker, good to see you again."

"Thank you, sir. It's good to see you."

"Oh, you two already know each other?" Mrs. Holloway asked.

"We do. Officer Tucker and his partner take turns patrolling the business area where the pharmacy is located, too."

"I'm sorry, Mrs. Holloway," Esther said. "I meant to tell you Sam came in the pharmacy the other day. You were out when I got home, and it slipped my mind."

"That's quite all right, Esther. But I am glad they've met."

"It's always good to know the policemen assigned to the area," Mr. Collins said. "But I think Sam is the first one to come in and introduce himself before something happened he had to come in and take care of."

"Have you had much trouble, Mr. Collins?" Emma asked.

The older man shook his head. "Not a lot, although I did have a break-in several years back."

Andrew entered the parlor just then and greeted everyone, shaking the men's hands and making his way over to Esther's side. The look the two gave each other caught Sam off guard and made him realize how badly he missed having Ann by his side, and in spite of his determination never to fall in love again, just how much he longed for—

"Dinner is served, ma'am," Jones said from the doorway. Mr. Collins escorted Mrs. Holloway, and Andrew did the same for Esther of course.

Sam held out a hand to Emma, who was still sitting on the couch. "May I escort you to the dining room?"

"You may. Thank you, Sam."

"What about me?" Grace asked. "Sam has two arms. He can escort me, too."

"Grace—"

"I'll be glad to escort you also, Miss Chapman." Sam crooked his free arm for Grace to take and she did so, quite gracefully.

Emma shook her head and giggled. "That's my sister."

Emma had seen the expression on Sam's face when he looked at Andrew and Esther. It seemed to be one of both sorrow and longing, and her heart went out to him.

She could only imagine the heartache of losing a loved one as he had his wife. It had to be hard for Sam to be around a couple as in love as Andrew and Esther were. She'd gotten used to it and, while she longed for a love of her own, she trusted that the Lord would bring him into her life when the time was right. But still, one couldn't help but long for the kind of love those two shared.

The Sunday night supper was set out on the buffet for

everyone to help themselves before taking a seat at the table.

Grace went in front of them, and Emma and Sam were the last in line.

"This is some spread for a Sunday night," Sam whispered in her ear.

"It is."

There was thinly sliced roast turkey, ham, and roast beef; warm crusty rolls; and all the condiments one might want to add to them. There were cheeses of all kinds and scalloped potatoes and peas to go along with it. For dessert, there was a four-layer chocolate cake and apple and cherry pies.

"I think Mrs. Holloway has wanted an excuse to have company over for a while. She seems quite happy tonight."

"Could it be because Mr. Collins is here?"

"It might be," Emma whispered back. "We all think he's courting her, but they haven't come out and said for sure."

Grace had already seated herself, and Sam pulled out Emma's chair and seated her before taking the one in between the two sisters.

As Esther and Andrew whispered to each other, Emma saw Sam glance over and then look away. Sorrow glimmered in his eyes again, and Emma wanted nothing more at that moment than to erase it.

For now, she felt that instead of bringing her a beau, the Lord had brought Sam back into their lives because he needed friends, needed something to keep him from thinking of his loss and to help him look forward to the future again.

"Andrew, would you please say a blessing?" Mrs. Holloway asked.

"Of course."

They all bowed their heads and he began, "Dear Lord,

we thank You for this day, for all of those around this table. We ask You to be with us as we begin our endeavor to help the young people soon to be leaving the orphanage. Please help us to be a blessing to them and to help them with the changes their lives are about to take.

"Thank You for Sam and his idea and for bringing it to us so that we can help with it, also. Please help us to come up with ideas that will truly be worthwhile to the young people we want to help, and please guide us and direct us to that end. Most of all, please help us to instill in them the desire to turn to You in all they do. In Jesus' name we pray, amen."

"Amen," everyone at the table said in unison before beginning to eat.

Emma turned to Sam. "Have you thought any more about your plan? Or talked to Mrs. Robertson yet?"

"I have."

"Good. We can all talk it over after supper."

"I imagine you're glad to have this weekend over with at the telephone office?" Sam asked.

Emma laughed. "It was quite busy up until about an hour before my shift left. I figured everyone was finally getting ready for the ball. By then it was too late to change one's mind."

Sam nodded. "I've been called in to cover a ball or two in my off-hours before. Glad I wasn't called in on this one."

"You don't like them?"

Sam shrugged. "Let's just say there are things I'd rather be doing. What about you? Would you like to attend one?"

"Oh, I suppose every woman wonders what it would be like to be a guest at something like that. But it's not something I really think about too much, and I don't think there's a chance that I'll ever go to one. Besides, I'm quite happy with my life right now."

Sam nodded. "I'm glad."

Once everyone seemed to be through eating, Mrs. Holloway said, "Let's go to the parlor and have coffee there. You can all discuss the coming week and what you plan to do."

Sam pulled out Emma's chair and crooked an arm for her to take, just as Grace got up from the table and took his other arm.

Emma didn't know whether to be amused or irritated with her sister. Sam turned and smiled at Emma, giving her a wink.

He seemed to think Grace was amusing, and Emma supposed she was. Sometimes she wished she were as outspoken as her little sister was. And sometimes she wished her sister would just be quiet.

"All right, Sam, tell us what you've come up with," Andrew said.

"I've given things a little more thought, and I was concluding that we might want to do a teamwork kind of thing. After this first meeting, perhaps it would be better if we stagger our visits—two people one week and two the next, so that the young people get used to talking to all of us at some point. They can't have enough good role models interested in them. What do you all think?"

"I think that it is a fine idea," Mrs. Holloway said.

"I like the idea," Andrew said.

"You and Esther could go one Saturday evening, and Emma and I could go the next. Grace can go with whomever she chooses, if she wants to."

"That makes sense," Esther said. "And that way some of us would be there each week."

"That's what I was thinking," Sam said. "Then we could still have an outing together, maybe one Sunday afternoon a month? What do you all think?" He'd taken a seat beside

Emma and now he turned to her. "You won't mind being my partner, will you Emma?"

"Of course not." How could she object? Her only problem was in being too pleased that he'd asked. She didn't want to like Sam too much, didn't want to be as attracted to him as she could no longer deny she was. He was still a policeman. And that created problems she just didn't want to deal with.

Emma didn't want to have to worry about him becoming corrupted. But most of all she didn't want to worry about his safety.

"So, will that work for you, Emma?" Esther brought her out of her thoughts.

"I'm sorry. I—my thoughts drifted. What were you saying?"

"Since we're coming up on the last weekend of the month, why don't we all go over this Saturday evening and meet everyone, give them a chance to meet us all as a group?" Sam asked.

"That should work fine for me if it works for the rest of you," Emma said.

"If you hadn't been woolgathering, you'd know it works for everyone else," Grace said.

"We all lose our train of thought occasionally, Grace," Esther said.

"I suppose. But I might wait to go along with you until you've had a chance to get everything established. I think I'll be more comfortable that way."

"I'm glad we can all make it." Sam got the conversation back on track. "It will give us a chance to explain what it is we'd like to help them with. And Grace, you can decide to come with us anytime you want. But as we don't exactly know how it's going to all work out, it might be best to wait. Then you can explain it better to those your age."

"All right," Grace said. "It will give you time to work the kinks out of your plans."

"Yes," Esther said. "And I do think we should make sure everyone knows that it's not mandatory that they meet with us—but that we'd just like to help."

"Do you think they won't want to meet with us?" Andrew asked.

"There might be one or two who are determined to go it on their own," Emma said.

"But if the others think they are getting something out of it, they might come around," Sam said.

"Exactly." Emma was glad Sam understood what she was trying to say. Of course, he'd lived in the orphanage and knew what it was like contemplating getting out on one's own. It was a mixture of excitement and pure fear. Andrew had never experienced anything like it, so he wouldn't know.

"I think it will work," Mrs. Holloway said. "They know most of you. I don't think they'll turn away your help for that reason alone."

"I'm eager to hear what happens," Mr. Collins said. "I think it's a fine thing you young people are doing."

"Yes, so do I. I'm very proud of you all," Mrs. Holloway added.

"Well, I suppose there's not much else to do except get started," Emma said. "Then we'll know more what it is each one needs most."

"You know, they probably are going to need help finding places to live. But they're going to need jobs before they can stay anywhere."

"I think some of them have begun to look for jobs, or have them already. At least that's what Mrs. Robertson has told me," Sam said.

"I can ask around at some of the businesses around

mine," Mr. Collins said. "And I could probably use another delivery boy and someone to help in the stockroom."

"That would be wonderful, Mr. Collins," Esther said.

"You know, I think I'll ask some of my friends if they know of any positions, too," Mrs. Holloway added.

"I'll ask if there are any openings at the telephone office. Someone is always getting married and leaving," Emma added.

"I knew I was doing the right thing enlisting help from all of you," Sam said. "I can't thank you all enough for agreeing to help out. I think we're going to really make a difference for these young people."

"We're going to try," Emma said.

"And we'll pray."

"That's the most important thing we can do," Mrs. Holloway said.

Emma couldn't agree more. She'd pray this worked out for everyone—and kept Sam very busy in his free hours.

Sam was pleased when Emma walked him to the door that evening. He'd been disappointed not to be able to meet her trolley as much as he'd thought he might in the past week, and he'd hoped to have a little time with her before he left that evening. He wanted to know how her week went.

For once, even Jones was absent from the foyer.

"It went well, don't you think?" he asked Emma as they stepped outside.

"I do. It is going to be very rewarding for all of us."

"Most of my friends from the orphanage have been gone awhile. Still, I remember a few as youngsters who used to listen to every word I said." Sam chuckled. "I hope they'll listen to me now."

"I'm sure they will. You were a role model for many of them," Emma said.

She looked up at him, and Sam saw something in her eyes.… But he couldn't quite read what it was. For a moment he thought he'd seen trust shining in them, and then they clouded over. Was it doubt he saw now?

"Emma, I have a feeling that you don't totally trust me, and I know you don't like that I'm a policeman. But I promise you, I want to help those young people about to be out on their own."

"I believe you, Sam. I just—" She broke off and shook her head. "I want to help, too."

He sensed she'd been about to say something else but changed her mind. Maybe one day she would trust him. He prayed so. And now, just to get Emma to trust him became a new goal. Maybe he just needed to spend more time with her. If she really got to know him, she'd know he wasn't going to let anyone corrupt him. But she only knew what she'd seen of him in the orphanage, didn't know who he was now, and probably thought he didn't care about those left behind…after all, he hadn't come back to visit or check on anyone.

And no one could deny that some corruption still existed in the police department. Sam certainly couldn't, and he wouldn't even try to convince Emma that it was all gone. But he did pray that things would continue to change for the better and that he could help those changes take place.

"I know you do. And you're going to be a great help. There is no doubt in my mind that we have a great group started. You know, if this works as well as I hope it does, maybe we can get something similar started at other orphanages in the city."

"Oh Sam, that would be wonderful. I'll be praying that

it works out for us and we can convince others to do the same thing."

Her eyes were shining bright, and Sam wanted to keep the happy look in them. "So will I."

"I guess I'd better go back in before Mrs. Holloway sends Jones out here looking for me. Or worse. She might send Grace."

Sam threw back his head and laughed. "That sister of yours is quite blunt, isn't she?"

"Oh, she is that, to be sure." Emma giggled. "Sometimes I wish I had a little of her outspokenness."

"You manage to get your point across quite well, just in a different way," Sam said. "You're fine just the way you are."

"Thank you, Sam. That is a nice thing to say."

"It's true." He looked down at her. She was a very special young woman. "You know, your parents would be very proud of you and Grace. Esther's would be proud of her, too."

Her eyes glistened in the moonlight. Maybe he shouldn't have said anything, but—

"And that was even nicer. Thank you, Sam," Emma said. "I'd better go in now."

"Yes, I suppose so. I'll see you before long."

"By Saturday anyway. You have a good week."

"You, too." Sam watched her slip back inside, wishing they could have talked a little longer. Only then did he realize he hadn't asked about how this past week had gone for her. Hopefully he'd see more of her this week and find out how it was going.

Chapter 9

By Wednesday, Emma found herself counting the days until Saturday, for it seemed she wasn't going to see Sam until then. And she was frustrated at herself because she wanted to see him.

She kept telling herself that she just wanted to make sure he was safe—she wasn't even sure where he lived or whom to ask to make sure he was all right. But she knew there was more to it than that. Sam made her feel…special, in a way she'd never felt before.

She'd never felt quite so confused in her life. All she knew was that she liked seeing him and talking to him very much. But she didn't like the way her pulse raced when he smiled at her, or the way her heart skittered in her chest when she spotted him waiting for her at the trolley stop. Just like it did now, when she stepped off the trolley and found him smiling up at her.

Emma couldn't have contained her smile if she'd tried.

She seemed to have no control over her reaction to seeing him again. "Sam, I was beginning to wonder if you'd been transferred to another beat."

He laughed and fell into step beside her. "No. I haven't been, but I did work several evenings I wasn't expecting to. One of the men on the night shift had to take his wife to the hospital."

"I hope she's all right?"

"She's fine. She had a bouncing baby boy—their first child."

"Oh, that is a very good reason for him not to come to work. I'm glad the mother and baby are all right."

"Yes, so am I."

But Sam's tone sounded wistful to Emma, and she had to remind herself that he'd been married and probably planning to start a family himself not so long ago. She didn't really know what to say. If she brought it up, it might bring sad memories back to him, and the easiest thing to do seemed to be to not mention it at all.

"How has your week been going?" he asked. "Any fancy balls coming up this weekend?"

She laughed. "Oh, I'm sure there are several, but evidently not quite as important as the one last weekend. And certainly none garnering the same kind of interest as that one did."

"So, it's been calm at work?"

"Fairly."

"What's been going on at home?" he asked.

"Oh, more planning for Esther's wedding of course. That never ends. And we have a women's suffrage meeting at Mrs. Holloway's tomorrow night. Life is never boring at home."

Sam's brow furrowed. "A women's suffrage meeting? At Mrs. Holloway's? You're involved in all that?"

From his tone it was obvious he didn't approve, and Emma turned to him. "Don't tell me you're against women having rights, Sam. Surely not!"

"Did I say I was against any of that?"

"No, but—"

"But a lot of people are, Emma, and these meetings are sometimes a dangerous place to be."

"We know that. But so far, nothing bad has happened at any of the meetings we've been to or held. And the one at Mrs. Holloway's isn't a huge group anyway."

"Still—"

Emma sighed and shook her head. "Sam, this is important to us—including Mrs. Holloway. But as for Esther, Grace, and me, you of all people should understand why being able to vote in elections that affect us as much as they do a man is important to us."

"I can understand it, Emma. But I don't want any of you hurt because of it."

"Sam, we aren't in danger. Besides, Andrew is at most of the meetings—and even Mr. Collins has come on occasion. You are welcome to come, too."

"Maybe I will."

"Maybe you should," Emma challenged. By then they stood at the front steps. "Want to come in and ask the others about the meetings?"

"I'd love to. But I'm still on duty and have to get back to work."

"I see."

Sam smiled at her and shook his head. "I'm not sure you do."

"Are you wanting an argument today, Sam?"

"No ma'am, I'm not." He grinned. "Are you?"

Emma felt disgruntled and wasn't even sure why. "Of

course not! The meeting is at seven tomorrow evening, if you can make it."

"I'll see what I can do."

"Good."

"I can't promise, Emma."

"I understand." But she wasn't sure she did. He didn't have anything else to do at night if he wasn't working. Or did he? That thought didn't help her mood at all.

"But I will see you soon, even if I don't make the meeting. I'd better go now."

"Have a good evening, Sam."

"You, too." He tipped his hat and turned to go.

Emma watched him walk away, and something about his walk and their talk had her wanting to call him back, but he was on duty and she couldn't get him in trouble.

Her heart gave a little twinge as she watched him round the corner and walk out of her sight. "Dear Lord, please keep Sam safe in all ways. Please keep him Yours. In Jesus' name, amen."

When Emma asked him to come to the suffrage meeting at Mrs. Holloway's, Sam hadn't been sure he could attend one because of his job. But he talked to his supervising officer and found that he would be allowed to go as long as he did it undercover as a police officer, in case something should come up that he had to take care of in his capacity as a policeman. He'd been warned not to tell anyone that he was undercover.

"We need to know who regularly attends these meetings so that we can recognize someone trying to disrupt them or bring harm to any of the women there," the officer had said.

So when Sam approached the Holloway house, a mixture of emotions washed over him. He was relieved that he was breaking no rules by coming to the meeting, but he didn't like the fact that he couldn't tell those he cared about he was actually working.

Jones opened the door before he could raise his hand to ring the bell, as usual. "Mr. Tucker. Good to see you. Miss Emma said you might be coming tonight."

"Thank you, Jones. It's good to see you, too."

"Everyone is meeting in the parlor. We have a few new people tonight, and I'm glad that we have you." He leaned a bit closer and said. "I always worry about the ladies here when there are meetings. Of course, Mr. Andrew is here tonight and Mr. Collins may show up. But it relieves my mind to know we have a policeman of your caliber in the mix, too."

"Thank you, Jones. Have you had any problems before?"

Jones shook his head. "No sir. But I worry that it is only a matter of time until we do."

The doorbell rang, and Jones motioned him to the parlor. "Go right on in, sir."

"Yes, I will. Just let me know if you spot anyone who looks suspicious to you. But don't let anyone else know. No need to worry them needlessly."

"Yes sir." Sam turned away as Jones answered the door.

"Good evening, Mrs. Ames. Mrs. Holloway will be pleased you were able to make it tonight," Sam heard him say as he reached the parlor.

The pocket doors between the front and back parlors had been opened up, and extra seating had been brought in. There were at least thirty people already seated. Emma rushed up to him with a smile that dived into his heart and made him glad he'd come.

"You did make it," she said. "I really didn't think you'd come."

"I figured it was about time I found out more about the cause." Of course he'd read about it in the papers, but most of that was negative. He was curious to know more.

"I, for one, am glad you came," Andrew said from behind him as he clapped a hand on his shoulder. "There are other men who come from time to time, but it's always good to have a friend in the mix."

Sam chuckled. "I'm glad to see you, too. I'd be feeling pretty awkward about now if you hadn't shown up."

The only seats left were in the back near the door, and that suited Sam fine. That way if anyone did cause problems, hopefully he'd be able to stop them before they could escape. He and Andrew took seats next to the back wall while Emma hurried forward to a seat saved for her near the front with Mrs. Holloway, Esther, and Grace.

Mrs. Holloway stepped up to a podium and welcomed everyone before introducing the speaker, a Mrs. Wainwright. Sam thought he'd heard of her before, probably from the newspapers, but he couldn't be sure.

"Thank you, Mrs. Holloway. For opening your home once more and for supporting our cause," Mrs. Wainwright began.

A round of applause sounded before Mrs. Wainwright held up her hands for it to stop and began speaking. "I know it may not seem so in our little corner of these United States, but our cause is gaining momentum all over our land."

She was a very demonstrative speaker, speaking with her hands as well as her voice, and Sam found himself listening to the words coming from her heart.

"It may take us many more years before we accomplish what we've set out to do. It may take a lifetime for some of us. But we *will* accomplish it. We *will* have the right to vote right along with our men. We *will* have a say in who governs this country we love just as much as any man does."

What she said made sense to Sam. Emma and the other women here should have that right. Especially those who had to look after themselves, with no man to help.

"We *will* have a say in what concerns our daughters and their daughters—our very own granddaughters. More even than ourselves, *they* are who we are fighting this fight for."

Mrs. Wainwright took a sip of water and continued, "Many of us already have daughters, nieces, and daughters of friends fighting the battle along with us. We will do it peacefully, amid all kinds of strife, amid all manner of discrimination. But we will not rest until we have the right to vote."

She wound up her speech by saying, "We will fight the battle, but we need more soldiers in this army. Continue to tell your family, your friends, and your acquaintances. Invite them to our meetings. Tell them the newspaper coverage doesn't tell the truth. Not all suffrage groups are trying to disrupt with their rallies. Our group isn't trying to fight current social issues as some are. We've decided to concentrate on the right to vote—to have a say in who our elected officials are. Only by attending and being involved can they know what we are truly working for. And pray, ladies. The good Lord is listening to us. We will have the right to vote one day."

The applause was loud and long, and Sam found himself clapping along with Andrew and everyone else. There was nothing he could find to complain about here. No yelling and fighting to have a say.

There were refreshments in the dining room, and he and Andrew lagged behind as the women headed that way.

Emma stopped in front of him on her way out. "What did you think?"

Her eyes were sparkling, as if she knew what he was going to say.

"There wasn't a thing I didn't agree with."

"I knew it!"

"But—"

"But?"

"That doesn't mean that I like the danger you women put yourselves in at these meetings."

"Sam—"

He held up his hand. "Please let me finish, Emma."

"Of course." Her words came out a little stiff, and he knew she was displeased with him.

"You can't blame me for worrying. You do the same thing about my work."

She opened her mouth to speak and then quickly shut it.

Andrew chuckled. "I think he has you there, Emma. All of you worry about Sam's work."

"I—" She broke off, shook her head, and chuckled. "I suppose you're right. We do."

Esther reached them just then. "What is he right about?" Andrew pulled her hand through his arm. "Come on. I'll tell you over a glass of lemonade."

"Would you like some refreshment, Sam?" Emma asked. "You did make an effort to come. Mrs. Holloway would be appalled if I sent you away without a snack of some kind."

Sam would rather just talk to her about the dangers of these meetings, how many meetings were broken up by men who did not want their women to have a say in the way government was run—how their families were run or even in their personal lives. But he knew she wouldn't listen to what he had to say. The way she felt about his being a policeman would only bring on warnings from her to him. Instead, he'd just enjoy her company for a bit. "I'd love some refreshment."

He crooked his arm, and this time she didn't hesitate to take it.

"Come this way."

Many of the women were on their way out the door before he and Emma reached the dining room. Sam supposed they had families they wanted to get home to and was a little relieved that by the time they made it to the buffet that'd been laid out, there were only a few small groups standing around talking with each other.

Emma handed him a small plate, and as they made their way around the table, she filled his plate with a few small tea cakes, some cookies, and fruit.

"Why don't you get us a glass of lemonade and we'll take these back to the parlor."

Somehow the extra seating had been taken away and the pocket doors between the two rooms had been closed. Everything looked normal again, and Sam was sure Jones had overseen getting the room back to the cozy atmosphere Sam enjoyed each time he came into the room.

Emma motioned for him to take a seat on one of the sofas, and he was a little surprised when she sat down beside him.

"Tell the truth, Sam. What did you really think of your first suffrage meeting?"

"I thought it was fine. The speaker was very passionate about the cause, and I admired the way she got her point across."

"You did?" Emma sounded surprised.

"I did. Emma, I don't have a problem with you wanting to get to vote. I do understand that. But at one time the group was trying to get many other issues included—

women's health concerns, divorce rights, and other such things. The things that stir up everyone and cause riots."

"I know. But *this* group is concentrating on only one thing now and that is getting the right to vote."

"Does everyone out there know that? All of those people who've been against the movement?"

"I don't know, Sam. I would think they do."

"You are much too naive, Emma. The people who are against any kind of women's rights are bound and determined to stop them, to cause trouble for them. And that is what worries me."

"I do agree with Sam on this," Andrew said as he took a seat on the sofa across from them. He and Esther had come into the room unnoticed, and now Sam turned to him.

"Thank you. I just want everyone to be aware of strangers who show up here and even at the larger meetings you might attend."

"That does make sense," Esther said. "You just want us to be watchful in case there is anyone ready to start trouble."

"That is it, exactly. I'll try to be here when you have a meeting here. And I know there are policemen on duty at the larger public meetings. But…"

"But?" Emma prodded him to go on.

"There still are pockets of policemen who might have been paid off to stand aside and let—"

"Are you admitting there is still corruption in the department, Sam?"

"I've never said there wasn't, Emma. Only that it is getting better. In fact, if you are at a meeting and see anything like that happen, it would be helpful if you tell me so that I can report it. Or if there is a policeman you can trust there, tell him what you saw."

"A policeman we trust, Sam? You are the only one who might even come close to fitting that description."

Sam didn't miss that Emma had said "might." She still wasn't sure of him. What was it going to take to gain her trust?

Chapter 10

Sam was working his business district on Friday afternoon and didn't get to see Emma, but he kept telling himself that he had the next day to look forward to. They'd firmed up their plans on Thursday evening after the meeting, and he met Emma and Grace, who'd changed her mind and decided to join them, along with Esther and Andrew, at the orphanage at dinnertime on Saturday.

Mrs. Robertson had insisted they eat there with the others. Once they were at the table, Sam realized it was a very good idea on her part. It felt like old times sitting at the long table with her and the older orphans.

Grace sat with the younger ones at a table adjacent to theirs—all except for the newest orphan—a baby of about a year old or so who'd been dropped off the week before. She was happily ensconced in Emma's lap now. Emma looked quite natural holding and feeding the baby while they had dinner.

Even Andrew seemed quite comfortable in these surroundings. But then, he had been here before. Emma had told him that Andrew visited with them from time to time and had even been called on to treat some of the children when they were sick. It seemed part of his time in practice was spent helping those less fortunate. Sam was glad he and Esther had found each other.

Once dinner was over, the younger children were sent off to the back parlor or up to their rooms, whichever they preferred, while the older ones joined Sam's group and Mrs. Robertson in the front parlor. Emma released the baby to the care of one of the older girls to put to bed, but Emma seemed quite reluctant to do so.

At dinner, Mrs. Robertson had introduced them to all the young adults who were getting ready to be out on their own soon, and now Sam concentrated on putting the names with the faces. Walter was no problem of course; he'd met him earlier when he'd come to the orphanage. And he remembered Carl and Jacob, too. The girls were a little harder to recognize because they'd changed so much, from young girls to young women, it seemed.

There was Caroline with curly brown hair, and Betsy with blond hair. Margaret had dark brown hair and Sally's was brownish red. They were all around the same age as Emma, but somehow she seemed more mature.

Everyone seemed quite pleased that those whom they'd looked up to were willing to help them now, just as they'd all hoped they would be. Sam was reassured to hear that several of them had already started looking for jobs.

Caroline had been hired as a nanny for the sister of one of her teachers.

"She's expecting her first child this summer, and I'll be moving in with them right after. They are very nice," Caroline said.

"That's wonderful, Caroline," Emma said. "I'm sure Mrs. Robertson gave you an excellent recommendation."

"I did," Mrs. Robertson said. "She's been a blessing helping with the younger children. She'll make an excellent nanny."

"So the rest of you know, we're asking around to find job openings you might want to apply for," Emma said.

"Yes. And my employer, Mr. Collins, said that he could use someone to work in the stockroom and deliver medicines at the pharmacy, if any of you are interested in that," Esther said.

"I might be interested in that," Carl said. "When can I apply?"

"I'll find out," Esther said.

"And Esther and I could use a receptionist at the office. It's taking too much time from my nurse."

"Oh, I'd love to be a nurse," Margaret said.

"They do have schools for that. Would you be interested in that, Margaret?"

"Of course I would, but I can't afford it."

Sam watched as Andrew and Esther exchanged a look, and when Esther gave her future husband a slight nod, he said, "Let me look into that."

"I might be interested in the receptionist position. I can type," Betsy said.

"That would be very helpful. We can talk more about that next week," Andrew said. "Esther and I will talk over hours and know more what it is we're needing by then."

The girl's smile was huge as she nodded. "I'm looking forward to next week even more now."

"What about you, Sally?"

"I don't really know what I want to do. Only that I need to work and find a place to live. I'm thinking about applying at Macy's and several of the department stores on Ladies' Mile. I like being around people, and"—she smiled and shrugged—"I think I'd like working as a sales clerk."

"If I hadn't gotten hired as a telephone operator, I would have done the same thing," Emma said.

They all chatted a bit more, with everyone getting to know each other better. All in all Sam was pleased with how well everyone had taken to the plan.

Maybe it was being able to talk to others not all that much older than them, knowing they were making it after they'd left the orphanage, but they all seemed quite comfortable talking to each other. By the time they left the orphanage, Sam felt they all had formed a bond he hoped would last.

"I think that went over well," Andrew said. "They all seem willing to talk to us."

"And to listen to what we have to say. I think they know we truly want to help them," Emma said. "And that you've already given them some job opportunities doesn't hurt."

"You know most of them," Sam said. "Do you think they'll be reliable workers?"

"Oh yes, I do. They all know they must work, and they've known that for a long time. I think they are just very excited about it—all except for actually moving out. It has to be intimidating to think of living alone."

"I know. I'm so glad we didn't have to do that," Grace said. "I'm going to give Mrs. Holloway a huge hug when we get home."

"We are blessed," Emma said. "But we do need to talk about that next time. Of course, I'm sure they know about the YWCA and the YMCA. Mrs. Robertson has given them that information, I know."

The night had turned chilly, and they were happy to find that Mrs. Holloway had cocoa waiting for them when they got back to her house.

True to her words, Grace gave her benefactor a huge hug.

Sam looked on as Mrs. Holloway hugged her back. "Is something wrong, dear?"

"Oh no. I'm just so thankful that we haven't had to worry about being out on our own. I think I take you for granted sometimes, and I don't ever want to do that. Thank you for taking us all in so we could stay together and not have to worry so much about the future."

There were tears in Mrs. Holloway's eyes when she looked at each girl. "You are more than welcome. But it is I who need to thank you all for enriching my life so much by letting me be a part of yours."

"I think we're all blessed in all kinds of ways," Esther said. "If not for you taking me in, I wouldn't be engaged to Andrew—wouldn't even know him."

Andrew shuddered, moved closer to his intended, and put an arm around her. "I don't want to even think about not knowing you."

The look the two exchanged had Sam missing what he'd lost and longing for someone to love now.

Emma was a little sad Sam hadn't been able to make it to Sunday night dinner the next evening. When he'd left the night before there was a look in his eyes that had her wanting to reach out and comfort him.

He'd seemed so...lonely when he left. She'd watched him as he looked at Andrew and Esther. His expression had changed then, and she was sure it was because he missed his wife so much. Even if she did find herself attracted to him she didn't want to come in second place to the woman he'd first loved. And it was obvious he had loved her.

Still, this was Sam, and she wanted to be a friend to him, wanted to make sure he didn't get caught up in the corruption of the police department, wanted to make sure he stayed safe and had things to do and people to spend time with so that he didn't get too lonely or depressed.

She'd been so impressed with him the night before when they were at the orphanage. She had no doubt that he was serious about helping those young people have an easier time adjusting to the changes coming their way, and she was glad to be helping. It made her feel a little less guilty for having such an easy time adjusting to life outside of the orphanage.

He was still on her mind on Monday, and she was thankful for work. She stayed busy enough that she had little time to think about Sam. He was taking up way too many of her thoughts lately and was sometimes becoming a distraction from her work.

Just as he was now. Several lights lit up on Esther's board, and in her hurry to get to them, she accidentally pulled the plug to a call in progress, hearing one side of the conversation.

"Joe, you go on and tell the others. We'll be at that meeting this week and we'll put a stop to it. Joe—Joe!" Esther held her breath. What was this man talking about?

There was a *click-click* on the line, and then the man was yelling, "Operator! Operator, are you there?"

"I'm so sorry, sir. You seem to have been disconnected. Would you like to be reconnected? Now?"

"Yes! At once."

"And who was it you'd been connected to?"

"Don't you know?"

"I'm sorry, sir. I just got back from lunch and—"

The man heaved a loud sigh over the line. "Connect me to 2338."

"Yes sir, immediately." Emma quickly reconnected the pin in the jack and breathed a sigh of relief when the lamp went out and the connection held. But it didn't stop her from thinking of what she'd just overheard. What meeting had he been talking about? And what was it the men were going to put a stop to?

When Emma got home that evening, it was to find Mrs. Coble, the seamstress Mrs. Holloway had hired to make Esther's wedding trousseau, ensconced in one of the extra bedrooms. She would be staying until she'd made all of Esther's clothing and the dresses Emma, Grace, and Mrs. Holloway would be wearing to the wedding.

Emma had never had anything made specifically for her, and she had tried to convince Mrs. Holloway that there was no need to go to that kind of expense for her—as had Esther of course. But Mrs. Holloway was determined, and there was no arguing with her over it. "Mrs. Coble has agreed to do all of it at a very reasonable price, and frankly, she needs the money. Her husband passed away not long ago, and this is the way she makes a living."

"Oh, I'm glad you've chosen her," Esther said.

"Good. She'll be staying with us—it will make the fittings easier on everyone with you and Emma working," Mrs. Holloway explained.

They were all introduced to Mrs. Coble at afternoon tea, and Emma was glad Mrs. Holloway had picked her. She was very sweet and had wonderful ideas, bringing along the latest fashion magazines and fabric swatches for them to pore over.

And pore over they planned to, right after dinner. Andrew didn't seem disappointed that he couldn't be in on this part of the wedding planning. Esther wanted her trousseau to be a surprise of course.

"I'll just go see how work is going on our apartment," Andrew said as they finished up the meal. "I didn't go by there after I went to the hospital, and I want to see how much they got done today."

Work on the apartment had begun only the week before, and he and Esther had looked in every day to see how things were progressing.

"It seems to be moving a little slow. I can't wait to see it finished just as we envisioned it," Esther said, taking a bite of the coconut cake Mrs. Holloway had made herself. "I'd like to go with you, but—"

"You know you aren't missing much just yet. A wall coming down here or there and others being put up."

"That's true. And I'm so excited to get my wedding dress started—"

Andrew grinned. "Is that a hint that I need to leave so you can get started?"

Esther laughed. "You know it isn't. But—"

"I'm on my way now," Andrew said as they all prepared to leave the table.

Mrs. Holloway led the rest of them to the parlor to give Esther and Andrew a few moments alone, and there was no way to ignore the slight flush on Esther's cheeks when she entered the parlor.

Grace giggled. "You look as if you've just been kissed, Esther. Were you?"

"It's none of your business, Grace," Esther replied.

"They are engaged, after all," Mrs. Holloway said. "Do you not intend to kiss your fiancé one day?"

"Why of course I do," Grace answered.

"If she's not too impertinent to be asked," Emma said.

Grace made a face at her. "And what if I should marry before you do, Emma? It could happen, you know."

Emma supposed it could. But she wasn't going to worry about it just yet. She shrugged her shoulders. "If you do, you do."

For once, her little sister seemed at a loss for words, and when everyone began to chuckle, even Grace joined in.

"Let's go over these patterns, girls, and see what we can come up with." Mrs. Holloway got everyone back on track as she began handing out magazines and the drawings Mrs. Coble had sketched out of her own designs.

"Oh, this is lovely," Esther said.

Emma looked over her shoulder to see a truly beautiful gown. It had simple lines and would look wonderful on Esther.

"Oh, it is," Emma agreed.

"It's of silk and lace. I can make it with long sleeves, or short and you could wear long gloves; the choice would be yours of course, as would be the fabrics we use," Mrs. Coble said, seeming pleased that they liked her design so much.

"I like this one, too," Grace said, holding up another of Mrs. Coble's designs.

Before long they'd all chosen their favorites, and all of them were all creations of Mrs. Coble's.

Then they all helped Esther choose the designs for the rest of her trousseau.

"This was easier than I thought it would be," Esther said. "I thought we'd be going back and forth with the choosing like we did the wall coverings and draperies for the bedrooms, Mrs. Holloway."

"Choosing one's own clothing is a bit easier, I think. We all have different styles we like and feel good in. And we all like different fabrics," Mrs. Holloway pointed out.

"And *that* might be a little more difficult," Mrs. Coble said. "Now that we have the patterns chosen, we can start thinking of different fabrics and colors. If I don't have enough swatches with me, I'll go out and bring in more tomorrow and we'll be on our way to having it all settled."

"Wonderful!" Mrs. Holloway said. "I'll have Jones bring us in some refreshment and we'll get started on those swatches."

By the time Andrew got back, they were in the middle of comparing silks and laces. Only his chuckle made them aware of his presence.

The women hurried to hide the designs and swatches they were looking at.

"Don't worry," Andrew said, "I won't come in. There's no need to put all your work up."

"No, it's all right. We've been at it quite awhile. We can move all of this up to Mrs. Coble's room now," Esther said. "We've picked the designs. Now all we have to do is choose more fabrics, but I certainly don't want you to see *any* of it."

"Not even a glimpse?" Andrew acted disappointed. "I've been in on all the rest."

"As you should be," Esther said, hurrying over to him. "But not this. This is all a surprise."

"All right, if you say so."

Emma watched Andrew brush an errant strand of hair behind Esther's ear, and she had no doubt at all that he would have kissed her cousin, if not in the presence of others.

Feeling as if she were intruding on a tender moment, she slid the pocket doors shut on the couple. "We'll just tidy up in here and then Andrew can join us."

There. That should give them a moment—if Jones didn't happen upon them. And Emma had no doubt that the butler was discreet enough that neither they nor anyone else would know. Something good to be assured of should she ever become engaged.

Suddenly Sam came to mind, and she tried to force the thought away, hurrying to help the others gather up the fashion plates, magazines, and swatches.

Chapter 11

Sam had tried several times to catch Emma at her trolley stop before he got off work in the mornings, but their hours were just too different or he was too far away to get to the stop on time.

After working a double shift earlier in the week, he was glad to have Friday off and was determined to see Emma. He wanted to talk over their plans for the next day with her and see if any of the young people had applied for the positions the others had mentioned.

So he made a point to meet her trolley Friday afternoon so he could walk her home and hope Mrs. Holloway would ask him to stay for dinner.

Emma's smile made the effort worthwhile, whether he would get an invitation to dinner or not. He smiled back as she stepped off the trolley.

"I was hoping to run into you today," he said.

"I'm glad you did. I've been wondering where you were,

but I suppose the night shift isn't an easy one and you must sleep at some point."

"I didn't used to mind it, but now I'd rather be working all days," Sam said, falling into step beside her. And he hadn't. Nights had always been the hardest for him after Ann died—the apartment seemed too empty and dark to him, and he'd hated spending time there other than to sleep.

But lately, it'd become easier to go home after spending time at Mrs. Holloway's or at the orphanage, and the apartment didn't seem quite so lonely now.

"I don't know how you do it—stay up all night. My stomach gets queasy if I stay up past around two in the morning or have to get up before five."

"It's not much fun, that's for sure. I don't usually get sick at my stomach though. I just find it hard to get to sleep when I work nights," Sam said. "But I usually don't go to sleep easily anyway."

"Do you read your Bible first? That always seems to help me."

"I did at one time. I'll try that again." He used to read his Bible every night, but he'd gotten lax in doing so and needed to get back into the Word. "Thank you for reminding me. I guess after Ann died the way she did, I had a hard time with that. Why the Lord would let it happen and all, and while I didn't turn away, my faith did get shaky for a while."

"How is it now?" Emma asked, the serious look in her eyes telling him she truly was concerned.

"It's much better. I still go to church with Ann's parents, and together we've worked through a lot with the Lord's help."

"I'm glad. I don't know how people get through the loss of loved ones or the disappointments in life without the Lord to turn to."

"No, neither do I." They walked in silence for a while. It was a comfortable silence, and Sam realized that Emma had a way of comforting him that she wasn't even aware of. He thought that Ann would have liked her a lot. He was sure that had they ever met, they would have been good friends.

As they neared Mrs. Holloway's Sam slowed his steps and Emma slowed hers. "Is something wrong, Sam?"

He shook his head. "No. I was just wondering if you think Mrs. Holloway would mind if I invited myself to dinner tonight? I'd like to talk over tomorrow with you and see if anyone has any news on the job situation for our young people."

Emma giggled. "Sam, they aren't all that much younger than we are. At least not than I am."

"I know. But I don't exactly know what to call them. Calling them children isn't right. And—"

"How about we call them our friends?"

He smiled. He should have known Emma would have the answer. "I like that just fine."

"Good. And I'm certain that Mrs. Holloway would be more than glad to have you stay for dinner. We've all been wondering where you were. Is there a way we can contact you if need be?"

The concern in her eyes washed over him, filling him with warmth at the knowledge that she and the others cared about him—and worried, too, if the expression in her eyes was what he thought it was.

"I'm sorry, Emma. Of course there is. I can give you the phone number of my landlady and the police department. I should have thought of it before now."

Her eyes sparkled once more, and Sam was glad.

"It's all right. As long as you give them to us before you leave tonight, all will be forgiven."

"I promise you, as soon as I have a piece of paper to write the numbers down on, you'll have them."

"And I will keep you to that promise," Emma said.

They'd arrived at Mrs. Holloway's and hurried up the steps just as Jones opened the front door.

"Good afternoon, Miss Emma, Mr. Tucker."

"Good afternoon, Jones," Sam said. It felt good to be welcomed into this house. He'd never thought he could feel as comfortable as he did here, but from the very first time he walked through Mrs. Holloway's door, he'd felt at ease.

And the greeting he received as he followed Emma to the parlor warmed his heart.

"Sam!" Grace's smile alone told him she was glad to see him. "I've been wondering when you were coming by again."

"It's always good to see you, Sam. Will you be able to take dinner with us?" Mrs. Holloway asked.

"I'd love to if you are sure you have enough."

"We always have enough for you, Sam," Mrs. Holloway said.

"I told you so," Emma whispered as they crossed the room.

She took the cup of tea Mrs. Holloway handed her.

"This one is for Sam, Emma dear." She poured another cup. "And this one is for you."

"Looks like you are still planning the wedding," Sam said as he spied the invitation samples laid out here and there over the tables.

"We are. You should have seen us earlier in the week when Esther was choosing patterns for her trousseau. We had fabric and patterns all over the place," Grace said.

"I suppose we should be doing this in the back parlor instead of here," Mrs. Holloway said. "But the light is better in this parlor during the day."

"And at least we got all the fabric swatches and patterns upstairs to Mrs. Coble's room," Emma said. "I do love my gown though. I can't wait for fittings to start."

"Mrs. Coble?"

"Yes, she's our seamstress," Mrs. Holloway said. "You'll meet her at dinner. She's busy cutting out Esther's wedding gown today. We finally decided on the fabric yesterday."

"She's staying here?" Sam asked.

"She is. She keeps on the go. Once she leaves here, she'll take her sewing machine to another home and make whatever it is they are in need of, then on to another. When her husband passed away, she lost her home, and this is the way she makes her living. And it provides her with meals and a nice roof over her head."

"I would imagine it would take someone who liked change in their life to be able to move around like that."

"Yes. I imagine she'll buy a home one day; but for now, she says this keeps her from being too lonely."

"I can certainly understand that reasoning," Sam said. He looked forward to meeting Mrs. Coble.

"And she does an excellent job. I'm sure she'll never lack for a place to stay."

Esther and Andrew came in just then and greeted him as if he were one of the family. Sam was beginning to wish he were.

Emma realized that the contentment she felt was because Sam was here. She didn't have to worry where he was or if he was safe at this moment, and she thanked the Lord for the peace that settled over her. She was also reminded of Sam's promise.

She hurried over to Mrs. Holloway's secretary and pulled a tablet out of the drawer along with a pencil and handed them to Sam. "You said you'd give us telephone numbers in case we need to contact you."

"Yes, I did." He smiled and took the tablet and pencil, quickly writing down several numbers before handing them back to her.

"Thank you," Emma said.

"You're welcome."

"I'm so glad Emma thought of that," Mrs. Holloway said. "There've been several times lately when I wanted to ask you to dinner and see how you are doing, but I wasn't sure how to get in touch with you."

"Now we do," Grace said, grabbing the tablet out of Emma's hand. "I'll make copies of it, so we all have one. You never know when you might need a good cop," she said.

"Do you have our number, Sam?" Mrs. Holloway asked.

"No ma'am, but I would like it, if you don't mind giving it to me."

"Grace, since you've commandeered the writing material, write our number down and give it to Sam, please," the older woman said.

"A lot of my customers just ask for the person, and after a while we know what line to connect, but we don't always know the number of the person they want to talk to," Emma said. "Mrs. Holloway might be known because this is *her* telephone number. But it'd be doubtful that another operator would know to connect to this line if you asked for me, or anyone else living here. So it's always best to have the telephone number if possible."

"How would one get in touch with Mrs. Coble, then, if she's always at a different house?" Sam asked.

"She keeps a schedule fairly far out and mails it to her clients," Mrs. Holloway said.

"That's right. I've found it works for me. And if the people I'm working with don't have a telephone, my clients

can contact me through the mail. I use a post office box."
Mrs. Coble entered the room with a smile. "Hard as it is
to believe for those who have them, there really are a lot
more people out there without telephones in their homes."

"Mrs. Coble, this is Sam Tucker. He's a good friend of
ours. Sam, this is one of the best seamstresses I've ever
known." Mrs. Holloway made the introductions.

"Pleased to meet you, Mrs. Coble," Sam said. She was
a slightly built woman who looked to be in her midfor-
ties to Sam.

"I'm pleased to meet you, too, Mr. Tucker. I'm enjoy-
ing getting to know Mrs. Holloway's new family a great
deal. I can see how they have enriched her life. There is
never a dull moment around here."

"I wouldn't think so with these three young ladies
around," Sam said. "They always have been full of life."

"And I'm blessed to have them with me," Mrs. Holloway said. "But I'm sure they've been missed a great deal
since they all left the orphanage."

"No doubt about that. And I'm very glad that we are
staying in contact with the others now," Sam said. "I know
I felt bad that I waited so long to go back. At least Emma,
Grace, and Esther have been much better at that than I
was."

"But you've remedied that, Sam," Emma said. "If not
for your ideas, we probably would have never thought of
the kind of help you've come up with."

"Dinner is served, ma'am," Jones said from the doorway.

"May I?" Sam asked as he crooked his arm to escort
Mrs. Coble to the dining room.

"Why, thank you, Mr. Tucker. It's been awhile since a
handsome young man has escorted me to dinner." She took
his arm and let him lead her to the dining room.

Emma laughed at the look on Grace's face as they followed Sam and Mrs. Coble into the room. "You know we don't own Sam, Grace," she whispered to her sister. "And did you see the look on Mrs. Coble's face? Sam did a very sweet thing just now."

"I suppose," Grace said, but Emma could see that she was as pleased with his treatment of Mrs. Coble as Emma was. Perhaps his heart went out to Mrs. Coble because he knew what it was to lose a mate. Emma couldn't even imagine, but she knew it must be devastating. And life would have to be lonelier after sharing it with another than if one had never married.

Sam had seated Mrs. Coble by the time Emma got to her chair, but he was waiting for her so that he could seat her also. Mrs. Robertson had made sure the children under her care knew how to be mannerly, and she'd be proud of Sam now.

More and more, Emma was beginning to believe that if anyone could be the kind of policeman this city needed, it would be Sam. Only now, as she'd barely begun to trust him, she worried more about him also and was afraid she was beginning to care more for him than she should. Even if he was the best policeman in New York City, he'd been in love with his wife and still missed her from what she could see. Could he—would he ever love another woman the same way?

Emma wanted to be loved with all of someone's heart—after the Lord of course. But she didn't want to come in behind a first wife. She needed to be careful of her heart, for it softened each time Sam smiled at her and she was afraid he was working his way right into it.

"How has your week been?" Sam asked, breaking into her thoughts.

"It's passed fine, except I did have something strange happen the other day."

"Oh?" Sam took a piece of chicken from the platter he'd been passed, held it for Emma to choose one for herself, and then turned to do the same for Grace. Jones took it from there and served Mrs. Coble.

"What happened?" Sam prodded.

"I'd just come back from lunch, and I accidentally pulled the wrong plug and disconnected a call in progress. And one of the callers continued to talk and…what he said was a little disconcerting."

"Why? What did he have to say?" Sam asked.

"He was talking to someone called Joe and said something like, 'tell the others.' "

"Tell them what?"

"About a meeting somewhere and that they would stop it. Then he evidently realized Joe wasn't there and he called his name. That's when I told him the call had been disconnected and asked if he wanted me to reconnect."

Emma saw Sam and Andrew exchange looks, and then Sam asked, "Do you by any chance remember the number or know who was calling?"

Emma closed her eyes and thought. "I believe it was something like 2833, or maybe it was…2338. I'm sorry, I can't remember for sure."

"It's all right. I'm just very curious to know what kind of meeting they wanted to stop," Sam said.

"I'd like to know, too," Andrew said. "Sounds like they want to make trouble for someone."

"Maybe I should have told my supervisor, but we aren't supposed to listen in on conversations. Still, it happens from time to time, and in an… Oh, I wish—"

"Emma, it's all right. But if something happens like

that again, maybe you could tell me, if you don't want to go to your supervisor?"

Emma wasn't sure what she should do. And yet, she didn't want to let anyone get away with a crime of some sort. "I'll tell one of you if I hear anything like that again."

Sam nodded. "Good. I don't want you to get in trouble at work, but you'd be surprised how many crimes are stopped by someone overhearing something."

"When we were little we were told not to be tattle-tales," Grace said. "I know it's important to tell certain things, but sometimes it's still hard to know when it's the right choice."

"Not necessarily as difficult as it seems, Grace," Sam said. "Not when it comes to a real crime about to happen. That's not quite the same as trying to get another child or sibling in trouble."

"That was earlier in the week," Emma said. "Have there been any reports of trouble at any meetings?"

"There are meetings of all kinds in this city. And trouble at some of them on a weekly basis. There'd be no real way of knowing which one might be a target on any given day, unless we know for sure when and where."

Emma felt disappointed in herself for not letting someone know what she'd heard sooner, but she didn't know how to fix it now. She stewed about it the rest of the night while they discussed their plans for meeting with the young people at the orphanage the next evening, and it was still in the back of her mind when Sam decided it was time to leave.

She walked him outside as usual, and when he turned to her, she found she hadn't hidden her feelings from him.

"You're still worried about what you overheard, aren't you?"

Emma nodded and sighed. "Oh Sam. I hope the fact that I didn't say anything didn't allow anyone to be hurt."

"Emma, even if you had said something, we might not have been able to stop anything. But if you hear something that worries you at all, be sure to let me or your supervisor know. Whomever you feel you should tell."

Emma nodded and prayed that she'd never overhear that kind of conversation again. "But will you try to find out what you can about any meetings being disrupted?"

"I will." He tipped her chin up so that she looked him in the eyes. "I promise. Try not to worry. You didn't know what to do or even what it was all about."

Emma released a sigh. "Thank you, Sam."

The fingers that had lifted her chin slid up to cup her jaw as he bent and kissed her on the cheek. "You're a good woman, Emma Chapman. I'm glad I'm getting to know you all grown up."

"I—" Emma stopped, her pulse racing and her heart pounding in her ears. She didn't know what to say.

Sam tapped her chin, turned, and started down the steps. "I'll pick you up at six tomorrow evening."

Emma found herself nodding even though he couldn't see her.

He turned back. "Is that time all right?"

She cleared her throat. "Yes, six is fine."

"Good." He smiled. "I'll see you then. You'd best go back in before Mrs. Holloway sends Jones to find you."

"Yes, I'd better. Good night, Sam."

" 'Night, Emma."

She turned and slipped back inside, glad that Jones was nowhere around. She placed her hand on her heart, willing it to slow its rapid beating. Sam had kissed her as he would have Grace—that's all. So why was her heart act-

ing as if she'd just received her first kiss from someone
she cared deeply about?

Perhaps because I just did? The thought had her pushing away from the door and hurrying back to the parlor as
fast as she could go.

Chapter 12

When Sam picked her up the next evening he acted as if nothing unusual had happened the night before, and Emma was surprised at how disappointed she was that he seemed the same as always. She didn't know what she expected or even how she wanted him to act, but whatever it was, he acted no differently than any other time they'd been together.

And it left her more confused than ever. She had been determined not to let herself have romantic feelings for him; and yet, last night she'd wished he'd take her in his arms and really kiss her. Not as he would Grace but as the woman he'd said she was.

Now, as they walked down the street to catch the trolley that would take them to the orphanage, she tried to hide her poor mood.

But Sam read her well. "You seem to be a bit out of sorts. Did you have a bad day?"

His concern touched her, and she shook her head. Obviously she wasn't doing a very good job of concealing her rotten mood. "No, not really."

"No?" He smiled at her in a way that seemed to ask a question.

"No." And she hadn't had a bad day. At least when she hadn't been thinking about Sam and wondering if he had any feelings for her beyond pure friendship. She was just aggravated with herself for letting her guard down and allowing her feelings for this man to begin to grow.

The trolley came to a stop just as they reached the corner, and Sam put a hand to her elbow to help her in. Then he moved over to allow her the window seat and sat down beside her.

"After we meet with the boys and girls—"

"Young men and women, or our friends," Emma corrected. "They aren't thinking of themselves as children right now."

"No, of course they aren't. Anyway, once we meet with them separately, perhaps we can join each other as one group for a bit and share any news they might have. Of course they've probably already shared that with each other."

"Not necessarily. If one got a job and the others didn't, they might keep the good news to themselves in order not to make the others feel bad. It wasn't easy for me to let them know I was moving in with Mrs. Holloway."

"Why do I always think you are older than the others?" Sam asked.

Emma's heart warmed at the thought that he did. At least he didn't seem to be thinking that she was too young.

"I don't know. Perhaps because I was already out and working when you found us again?"

"Perhaps. Or maybe—you looked quite natural holding the baby the last time we were at the orphanage."

"Oh, the new baby." Emma smiled just thinking about her. "Mandy is her name. Isn't she precious with those big blue eyes and curly hair? I've always had a weakness for the little ones at the orphanage. They'll never even remember their parents. It makes me so sad for them."

"Yes, me, too. But even before I saw you holding the baby, you've seemed more mature than the other girls your age. Maybe it's because you had Grace to look after, too?"

Emma shrugged and raised an eyebrow at him. "Are you saying I'm old, Sam?"

"At eighteen? I don't think so. But you just seem—" He grinned and shrugged. "I'm certainly not calling you old."

Emma giggled. "It's all right. I'm not trying to put you on the spot. I've always felt a little older than some of the other girls, and maybe it does have something to do with feeling responsible for Grace. Esther and I were so worried when the time was nearing for me to leave and Grace would have to stay behind. We will always be so thankful that Mrs. Holloway took that worry away."

"I'm thankful, too. I'd hate to think of Grace feeling all alone, although I don't think she would ever have let you know if she was miserable. She's tough."

"She is. And you're right, she would have kept her fears to herself."

"Being raised in an orphanage can make one tough. And I know that even without our help, these young people would probably make it, but I want to help the transition be easier than it might be otherwise."

The trolley came to their stop, and they hurried off and up the street to the orphanage. As before, Mrs. Robertson had dinner ready and waiting when they arrived. The baby seemed to recognize Emma and reached out to her.

Emma grinned at Sam as she took Mandy in her arms and sat down at the table with her. The baby's smile captured her heart, and Emma suddenly wished she were in a position to adopt her. If only single women could adopt a child.

As she jiggled the baby in her lap, taking turns feeding her and taking a bite of her own food, she realized there was something about sitting at the same table with others she'd been raised with that made conversation flow easily.

As they ate the hearty stew that had always been a favorite of Emma's, everyone caught them up with their week.

"Have any of you found work yet?" Sam asked.

"I applied at the drugstore Esther told me about, and I'll start training there this coming week after school." Carl grinned. "Mr. Collins has said he'll use me part-time until school is out, then I'll work full-time as a stockman and delivery man."

"That's wonderful news, Carl," Sam said. "Any others with good news for us?"

"I did apply at Macy's yesterday afternoon," Sally said. "They called Mrs. Robertson today to find out about me."

"And I told them she would make a wonderful employee," Mrs. Robertson said.

"Hopefully I'll hear from them next week," Sally said.

"Oh, I hope so, too. I'll be praying you get the position. Do you know what department you'll be working in?" Emma asked.

"No. But it doesn't matter. I just want to work there and will be happy anywhere they put me."

"With that attitude, I'm sure you'll move up in no time. You could be a department manager one day, Sally," Emma encouraged the young woman.

"Oh, I don't know about that, but I do think I'll like working there."

By the time they'd finished their meal and had separate meetings—Emma with the young women and Mandy, and Sam with the young men—she and Sam were pleased to see everyone seemed a bit less nervous about their futures than before.

Mrs. Robertson put the baby to bed before both groups joined each other in the parlor, and after playing a few games of charades, she and Sam took their leave.

"Now don't forget that Andrew and Esther will be here next Saturday," Sam said.

"You all have Mrs. Holloway's phone number in case any of you need to talk to one of us, don't you?" Emma asked.

"We do," Betsy said.

"Good. We'll see you soon."

After everyone said good night, Mrs. Robertson walked them to the door. "I can't tell you both how very proud I am of you. That you care enough to help others have an easier time moving on is something I'm very grateful for. They've seemed more relaxed this week. I was beginning to see the strain of worrying about what they were going to do on their faces, but knowing they have others to turn to has already made a difference. Thank you."

She pulled them each into a hug, and Emma had to blink back tears as she said, "No, it's you we have to thank—for being there for us and for being here for others now."

"Emma is right. You helped instill that kind of caring in us by making sure we know the Lord and teaching us about Him." Sam cleared his throat, and Emma could tell Mrs. Robertson's words had touched him, too.

"Go on, you two, or you'll have me bawling my eyes out soon." Mrs. Robertson motioned them to leave, and after one last hug, Emma and Sam hurried down the steps and toward the trolley stop.

"I don't think we appreciated her like we should have when we lived there," Emma said.

"I know I didn't," Sam said. "But I will be praying for her and the work she does from now on."

"Yes, so will I."

The night air had turned cooler, and Emma began to shiver as they waited for their trolley. She pulled her cloak a little tighter.

"Are you cold?"

"A little," Emma said just before the trolley stopped and they hurried on.

Even Sam gave a shiver as they took their seats. "It's getting colder out. Won't be long before the first snow."

"It's the end of September now. Wonder how long it will be before we can all go ice-skating?"

"Several more months probably," Sam said. "Depends on the weather."

"Maybe we can go as a group with our friends from the orphanage," Emma suggested.

"That's a good idea. We'll have to mention it."

Everyone was in the parlor when they arrived back at Mrs. Holloway's, including Mr. Collins who'd come for dinner.

A fire had been lit in the fireplace, and both Emma and Sam headed straight for it.

"Turning colder out, is it?" Andrew asked.

"It is." Emma rubbed her hands together.

"I'll have Jones bring us some cocoa."

"Oh, that would be wonderful," Emma said. She looked up at Sam. "It will warm you up before you have to stand at the trolley stop again."

"How did things go at the orphanage?" Esther asked.

They filled them in on their meetings and caught them up with what was going on at the orphanage.

"Sally thinks she has a position at Macy's," Emma said.

"And Carl told us that he's going to start at the pharmacy." Sam looked at Mr. Collins. "He seems very excited about it."

"Good. That's the kind of employee I need. He seems to be a fine young man."

"Yes, he does," Sam said. "I hope he works out well for you."

"I believe he will."

"I'm sure the others will find work soon, too," Sam said.

Emma told them all what Mrs. Robertson had said about the young men and women seeming more at ease about their futures.

"How wonderful. See, you are all making a difference already," Mrs. Holloway said.

"It's going to take all of us, but I think we are," Sam said, glancing down at Emma.

"So do I." Emma smiled at him. "And it was all your idea, Sam."

"But I can't do it alone, and I thank you all for agreeing to help."

"I'm just glad you asked us to. Next Saturday is Esther's and my turn, right?" Andrew asked.

"Right. And then we'll get together the next week as a group. Maybe a picnic at Central Park if the weather allows for it," Sam said. "Emma suggested we all go ice-skating once the lake freezes over."

"I like both those ideas," Esther said.

"I want to go ice-skating, too," Grace said. "I'll just go when you all do the group thing."

"You don't want to go with us next weekend?"

"No. I'm helping Mrs. Coble. She's teaching me to sew a bit. I think I know what I want to be."

"Oh? What?"

"I want to design and make clothes like she does, only I want to set up my own shop one day."

"You don't want to be an author?"

"Somehow I think I'd make more money designing clothes."

"Life isn't all about making money, Grace," Esther said.

"Oh, I know. But I think it might be hard to make enough writing. I'll save that for when I get old."

"If anyone can do it, you can, Grace," Sam said.

"That's true. And who better to learn from than Mrs. Coble?" Emma asked.

"Exactly," Grace said.

Mrs. Coble shook her head and smiled. "She learns fast and is a joy to have around."

"I suppose we'll have to settle with you going on our group visits, Grace," Sam said. "I'm sure everyone will be glad to see you then."

Jones brought the hot cocoa in just then, and Emma and Sam got the first cups. "Oh, this is delicious. Thank you for thinking of it, Mrs. Holloway," Emma said.

"Yes, thank you. It will warm me up for my walk to the trolley."

"No need for you to take the trolley, Sam. I'll drop you off on my way home," Mr. Collins offered.

"Are you sure you don't mind?"

"Not at all."

"Then I'll take you up on the offer, sir."

"Good."

Emma was a little disappointed she wouldn't get a few minutes alone with Sam when she walked him out. But it was cold out there, and she didn't want him to have to stand in it waiting for the trolley. It'd been a good day. She'd be thankful for it.

* * *

Sam was glad it'd warmed up a bit the next day. He'd attended church with his in-laws and then gone home to have Sunday dinner with them.

He filled them in on what was happening with his plan to help at the orphanage, and they seemed very glad that he was keeping busy.

"You said you had some of your friends helping, too?" William asked.

"Yes sir. There are three young women who are related—two sisters and their cousin who were orphans, too." He explained about Esther, Emma, and Grace and how he connected with them once more. "Esther is engaged to a doctor now, and they are both helping also. We've kind of formed a group to take turns visiting and trying to be there each week."

"I am so pleased, Sam," his mother-in-law said. "I know Ann would be, too."

For a moment he wondered if Margaret somehow knew he was beginning to feel more for Emma than just friendship. But of course there was no way she could. And they'd already told him that they would accept whomever he might fall in love with.

At the time he'd been certain he'd never fall in love with anyone again and he didn't want to. But lately he knew something was changing, and whether he wanted to or not, he was very close to falling in love with Emma Chapman. Seeing her with that baby had made his heart turn to pure mush. She'd make a wonderful mother.

He'd wished for a few minutes alone with her the night before, but Mr. Collins's offer of a ride home had been so generous, he couldn't refuse it. Besides, the man had gone out of his way to be kind and he'd hired Carl, too.

And Sam realized he'd be seeing Emma later for supper. He couldn't deny looking forward to seeing her again tonight.

"Thank you. It is good to be connected with them again, and those at the orphanage. It's good to feel we're helping others. And I know it will be good for them, too."

"I'm sure it will be. It's not good to lose touch with those whom we've shared our lives with. Remember, even if you should remarry one day, Sam, we consider you a son. And we'd very much like to have another daughter in our lives, too."

Sam closed his eyes against the pinprick of emotion in them. These were such wonderful Christian people. He was blessed to have them in his life. "I promise you both, that should I ever remarry again, you will still be family to me and to her, too. Always."

"Thank you, son. That's all we ask."

Emma enjoyed church that Sunday morning. The sermon was one on trust, and it captured her attention from the beginning. She realized that it was when she left things in the Lord's hands, trusting Him to guide her, that things seemed to work out best in her life.

And yet, she'd decided on her own not to trust Sam from the moment she found out he'd become a policeman. Just because he'd become a cop. How dare she judge him like that?

Oh, her opinion had begun to change over the time she'd gotten to know him better as an adult, but she knew now that it was God working in her to enable her to begin to trust Sam. And it was God she needed to put her trust in for her future—whether it had anything to do with Sam or not.

She did feel the Lord wanted them to be friends, if nothing more. They'd formed a bond because they were both orphans and they were trying to help others who'd lost their families. If there were to be more between them, then she needed to trust that the Lord would let her know and quit worrying about it all.

She went home with a renewed feeling of trust in the Lord to guide her and looked forward to seeing Sam that evening. They were friends, after all.

She found herself watching the clock all afternoon. She'd had the fitting of her maid-of-honor dress and then watched as Esther had her fitting. She was going to make a beautiful bride.

They'd spent the rest of the afternoon helping address invitations to the wedding.

"You did put Sam on the guest list, didn't you?" she asked.

"No."

"No? Why not?" Emma said.

"Because Andrew is going to ask him to stand up for him. To be his best man."

"He is?"

"I am," Andrew answered. "I've thought a lot about it. Most of my friends are in Boston, and I've come to like Sam a lot. I decided I'd like him to be my best man if he has no objections."

Emma smiled. "That's nice of you, Andrew."

"Do you think he'll accept?"

"I'm sure he will. And I'm so glad you like him. Sam could use a good friend."

"I think we all can, but they aren't always easy to come by."

"No, they aren't. When are you going to ask him?"

"Tonight."

Emma smiled and looked at the clock once more. Four o'clock. Two more hours until Sam got there. She hoped he was as happy with Andrew's decision as she was. With her as Esther's maid of honor, it seemed fitting that Sam might be Andrew's best man.

Chapter 13

After Sam's visit with Ann's parents, he felt at peace about the future. They trusted the Lord to guide them, and he needed to do the same. They would accept it if he fell in love and wanted to marry again, and he needed to quit feeling guilty that memories of Ann were being replaced by Emma.

He would always love Ann, but she wasn't here, and it was because he'd loved married life so much that he knew he wanted to be a husband again. Wanted a wife who would love him and be a good mother to their children, and he wanted Emma to be that person.

But if she still didn't trust him, how was he ever going to persuade her to give her heart to him? *Dear Lord, please help me to know how she feels about me. To know if my dream about having a life with her is even possible. I know I'm falling in love with her, but I need to know if she could ever feel the same way about me. Please help me to know. And if not, please help me to accept it and still remain friends with her. For she's made a difference in my life already, and I...don't want to lose her. In Jesus' name, I pray, amen.*

Sam went back to his apartment to change for supper at Mrs. Holloway's and found that he had a message from his partner to contact him as soon as possible. Sam did so immediately.

"Richard? My landlady said you needed to talk to me?"

"Sam, yes. I wanted to tell you that I found out there was trouble Friday evening at one of those suffragette meetings."

"Was anyone hurt?"

"Not badly this time. But it appears to be one of those groups who go around just trying to stir things up. Wish we could find out who it is sending them out."

"Yeah, so do I." He couldn't help but wonder if the call Emma had overheard had anything to do with this.

"If your friend overhears anything else—"

"I'm certain my friend will tell me or someone else who can help." Sam hadn't wanted to name Emma. He wanted her name to stay out of any conversations. He still wasn't always sure who he could trust either, and he didn't want anyone suspecting where he might be getting his information. Besides, he didn't really know if Emma would come to him or go to her supervisor if she did hear anything else.

"Good. Maybe one day we can put a stop to some of these troublemakers. I've told my wife she can't go to any of those meetings. Not that I don't believe she should have the right to vote, but because I don't want anything to happen to her."

Sam didn't want anything happening to Emma or the others at Mrs. Holloway's either. But he knew he didn't stand a chance of stopping Mrs. Holloway from holding a meeting—not one.

"Thanks for letting me know what you found out, Richard. I'll let my friend know. Maybe it will make it easier for…my friend to tell someone next time."

"I certainly hope so. Have a good evening, and I'll see you tomorrow."

"You, too." Sam hung up on his end and took the stairs two at a time to change. He didn't want Emma to feel guilty that she hadn't told anyone, but he did want her to know that she needed to. And if she told him, that'd mean she'd come to trust him. And maybe, just maybe, he had a chance of getting her to trust her heart to him. *Dear Lord, please let it be so.*

By the time Sam got to Mrs. Holloway's, Mr. Collins was arriving, too.

"Sam, I should have called and brought you over with me. I'll take you home this evening though. It's getting colder by the hour. I think we may have an early winter."

"Thank you, sir. I'm beginning to think the same thing." He actually hoped so. He'd love to take Emma ice-skating soon. The thought of gliding over the ice with her at his side put a smile on his face.

As usual, Jones opened the door for them before they rang the bell and took their overcoats once they stepped inside.

"Everyone is in the parlor. Supper will be ready shortly, gentlemen," Jones said.

"Thank you, Jones," Sam and Mr. Collins said at the same time.

They were welcomed into the parlor in a way that never failed to warm Sam's heart. Emma's smile reached into his heart and seemed to give it a little twist.

"Is it cold out? Your face looks a little pink from the weather. Come warm yourself by the fire."

She was standing in front of the fireplace, and Sam wasted no time in joining her there.

"It is cold," he said. "Mr. Collins and I were just talking about how it looks as if we might have an early winter."

"I hate for you to work out in the cold, and I certainly don't look forward to standing at the trolley stop in the cold, but I do like snow and skating at Central Park."

"We'll go as soon as we can," Sam said. He bent a little closer and lowered his voice. "I heard from my partner earlier. He found out that there was a raid of sorts on a suffragette meeting the other night."

"Oh Sam, I—"

"Now, there's no way to know if what you overheard had anything at all to do with it, so don't start feeling as if you are responsible for it in any way. I just wanted you to know that you might have heard something important enough to tell me or your supervisor, so if it happens again…"

Emma nodded, and he knew she understood what he was saying. No need to push any further. She'd tell someone. He only prayed it would be him.

"A telephone call for you, Mr. Andrew. It's Mrs. Robertson from the orphanage. She said it was important," Jones said from the door. "And supper is ready, ma'am."

"You all go on in," Andrew said. "I'll be there as soon as I finish the call."

They'd barely taken their seats when he rushed back in. "I've got to leave. The new baby, Mandy, is sick and Mrs. Robertson wants me to check her out. She's been running a fever and she can't get it to break."

Emma sprung up from her chair. "I'm going with you. Mandy has taken a liking to me and I might be able to help."

Andrew nodded. "Come on, then."

"I'm coming, too," Sam said. "I'm sorry to mess up your Sunday supper, Mrs. Holloway."

"Oh, don't worry, Sam. I totally understand. You all go on over and we'll keep things warm for you."

"If Andrew and you two are going, so am I," Esther said.

"I want to go—"

"Oh, please stay with us, Grace. We don't know what the baby has, and I don't want you to get sick."

"Mrs. Holloway is right, Grace. It could be something contagious that you haven't come down with yet. I think you should stay here," Andrew said.

The younger girl looked at Mrs. Holloway who gazed at her imploringly. She sighed and nodded. "All right, I'll stay."

Everyone quickly donned their cloaks, hats, and gloves before heading out to the hack Andrew had called for.

Emma's brow was furrowed, and Sam knew she was worried about the baby.

"How old is this little one, Emma?" Andrew asked.

"She appears to be a little over a year old. She seemed to be just fine when Sam and I saw her yesterday. I don't see how she could get sick so quickly."

"Oh, it happens with babies. More than likely she's teething or something simple like that."

"I pray that's all it is."

Emma bowed her head and Sam knew she was doing just that, praying for little Mandy. That Emma could care so much about a child who wasn't her own made Sam even more certain that she would make a wonderful mother and that he wanted her to be the mother of his children. He sent up his prayer that joined Emma's in asking for the baby to be all right.

When they arrived at the orphanage, it was to find Mrs. Robertson rocking the crying baby. The older woman looked exhausted, and when Mandy cried even harder when Andrew tried to take her, Emma hurried over.

The glassy eyes of the child told even Sam that she had a fever, but it was when she stopped crying and held out her hands for Emma to take her that he realized this child did have a very strong attachment to Emma.

Emma quickly took Mandy, and only then did the baby let Andrew come close. Emma held her while Andrew began to speak gently to the baby as he looked into her eyes and ears and then listened to her heart. With Emma's coaxing, he was able to look into Mandy's mouth and began to nod.

"It does appear that she's teething—cutting several at a time, from the looks of it," Andrew said. "I know many of my peers say babies don't run fevers when they are teething, but I don't agree."

"I thought that was it, but she wouldn't even let me get my finger in her mouth to check. Shut it tight or tried to bite me," Mrs. Robertson said. "Obviously, I'm losing my touch with babies."

"No, you aren't," Esther said. "She's just formed some special kind of attachment to Emma."

"Maybe she reminds her of her mother in some way," Sam suggested.

"That's what I was about to say," Mrs. Robertson said. "I'm just glad she's stopped crying for a bit. Poor baby, breaks my heart to hear her cry."

"I know. I'm going to leave some medicine with you." Andrew pulled a small bottle out of his medicine bag and handed it to Mrs. Robertson. "Just rub a little on her gums. It should ease her pain and give you both some rest, as it will make her sleepy."

Mrs. Robertson tried to take Mandy, but the baby jerked away and put her head on Emma's other shoulder.

"May I?" Emma asked.

"Yes, please. No need to upset Mandy by having me try to open her mouth again right now," Mrs. Robertson said.

Andrew used a dropper and put a bit of the liquid on Emma's finger. "Just gently rub her gums with it."

Whatever it was seemed to work quickly because Sam could see the child relax in Emma's arms.

"That should take care of her for tonight. But if her fever seems worse, telephone me. Otherwise, I'll stop by first thing in the morning," Andrew said.

"Thank you, Dr. Andrew. I will."

"I suppose we should be on our way," Esther said.

"You all go on. I'll take the trolley back. I want to stay until Mandy goes to sleep," Emma said.

As if he'd let her take the trolley alone this time of night! "I'll stay with you and see you home," Sam said.

"Do you mind?"

"No, not at all." He could watch Emma with that baby for the rest of the night, if need be. The way she gently patted Mandy's bottom as she held her, the little kisses she placed on her head, told him she was just as attached to the child as Mandy was to her. "I'll be glad to."

"We'll go on, then," Andrew said.

"It looks like she'll be asleep pretty soon," Esther said. "We'll tell Mrs. Holloway you'll both be along shortly."

Mrs. Robertson showed Andrew and Esther out.

"Thank you, Sam," Emma said. "I just couldn't leave Mandy yet."

"You're welcome. I understand and I'm glad you feel that way."

Her gaze moved from the baby to him. "You are?"

In that instant Sam imagined she was his wife and it was their baby she was holding, caring for.

"Sam?"

Her question brought his attention back to her, but the image in his mind stayed. "Oh yes, I'm sure."

Mandy stirred in her arms, and Emma pulled her gaze from Sam. Something in the look in his eyes set her pulse racing faster than lightning. For just a moment Emma felt a longing so strong she caught her breath.

Something about sitting in this room with just Sam and Mandy seemed right, but at the same time, it unsettled her. Her feelings for Sam seemed to grow each time she saw him, and she—

"Oh, look." Mrs. Robertson brought Emma out of her thoughts. "You've got her to sleep, and from the look on her sweet face, her pain has eased. I can take her now, or you can put her to bed, if you'd like. I've had her crib moved to my room so I'll hear her if she wakes."

"I'd like to put her down," Emma said. She didn't want to relinquish the baby in her arms to anyone else right now. Didn't really want to leave her, but she knew Mrs. Robertson would take excellent care of Mandy.

She followed the woman to her room and laid the child down in the crib. Mandy gave a little jerk, and Emma gently patted her long enough to soothe her back to a sound sleep.

Both women tiptoed out the door and went back downstairs.

"You are going to make a wonderful mother one day, Emma."

"Thank you. I hope so. Maybe I can telephone tomorrow to see how she's doing? I'll be glad to come back and give you a break if she keeps you up tonight."

"Thank you, dear. By all means, feel free to telephone me. And thank you for your offer. I think she'll sleep good tonight, now that her pain has eased."

Sam was talking to several of the young men when they got back to the parlor, but he stood as soon as they entered the room. "Mandy's all right?"

"She's sleeping," Emma said.

"Thank you for staying and getting her to sleep. She really has taken quite a liking to you, Emma. You come see her anytime."

"I will. She's kind of claimed a piece of my heart."

"I could see that."

"Yes, so could I," Sam said, looking down at Emma. "I think Emma is a natural nurturer."

"She is," Mrs. Robertson said. "You two best be on your way. Bundle up good; it's getting colder out."

Sam helped Emma on with her cloak, and she pulled the hood up over her head, grabbed her gloves from her pocket, and put them on.

"Good night," they called as they hurried outside so as not to let any more cold air in than necessary.

"I hope the trolley is on time. I hate for you to have to stand out in the cold," Sam said, pulling her hand through his arm and walking as close as was permissible.

"It's all right. The wind isn't blowing too much." Sam's arm felt warm, and he blocked what breeze there was.

They arrived at the trolley stop about the time it made it there, and they hurried on. The trolley was nearly full with only two empty seats left. Emma felt warmer the instant Sam sat down beside her.

"Better?" he asked.

"Much. Thank you for staying with me."

"There's no way I would have left you to come home by yourself after dark."

"I know." Emma told herself he was only doing what he thought was his duty and that it didn't mean anything that he was escorting her home. But what really bothered her was the realization that she suddenly wanted it to mean more.

As if he could read her thoughts, he leaned close to her ear and said, "And it has nothing at all to do with being a policeman."

Her heart fluttered, and she could feel warmth creeping up her cheeks as she told herself it only meant that he was a good man. Nothing more.

The wind had picked up by the time they got off the trolley, and they hurried to Mrs. Holloway's. Jones quickly opened the door for them, and Emma was glad to find that, true to her word, Mrs. Holloway had kept their dinner warm. She'd hate to send Sam back into the cold on an empty stomach.

Everyone joined them in the dining room while they ate.

"Emma got Mandy to sleep not long after the two of you left," Sam said to Andrew. "That medicine must have eased her pain quickly."

"I'm glad. She was exhausted, anyway. I'm sure she'll cut those teeth overnight or by tomorrow afternoon. I'll check in on her in the morning, and if she isn't better, I'll look in on her before I come home tomorrow," Andrew said.

"I hated to leave her," Emma said. "But Mrs. Robertson will take excellent care of her. I remember when Grace got so sick just after we were taken in, do you, Esther?"

"I do. We were so worried she had the same thing that took our parents."

Emma nodded. "We were. But thankfully, Mrs. Robertson nursed her through it. I don't think I realized then what a wonderful woman she was. I know we took her for granted, thinking she was just doing her job, but not understanding that she really did care about us."

"We owe her a debt of gratitude, that's for sure."

"I can tell you that helping with the older ones is helping to repay her," Sam said. "She really is so happy that we are doing that. It makes her feel better about them leaving."

"I'm glad we're keeping contact with them and with her," Emma said.

"I wish I had realized how much it would mean—not just to the orphans, but to her, to stop by once in a while," Sam said.

"She's a good woman," Mrs. Holloway said. "Both she and her husband were in charge when he was alive. She couldn't have children of her own, and they both loved them. It was a way they could have children in their lives and make a home for them."

"I didn't know that," Emma said.

Esther shook her head. "Neither did I. How wonderful for us that she's made it her life's work to take care of those who have no one. And from what I've learned about other orphanages, we've been blessed to have been sent to the Ladies Aide Society Orphanage."

"Oh, no doubt about that. I've seen many orphanages in the city," Andrew said. "I've let those near my office know they could call me. And sadly, some of them are horribly run, and of course they are all overcrowded."

"She's one of the few who've never sent anyone off on an orphan train."

"I remember lying in bed at night worrying about that and wondering if we would be separated," Emma said. "Mrs. Robertson could tell I was fretting over something and asked me what was wrong."

"What did she say when you told her?" Sam asked.

"She said she'd never separate us or send us away. Once

a child was under her care, she saw that they stayed with her, unless a wonderful family came to adopt them. But she promised that Esther and I were old enough to let her know if we wanted to stay or go and all we had to do was tell her."

"Yes, she assured me of the same thing. Of course, most people who adopt want a baby or a very young child. I know there aren't many orphanages run the way Mrs. Robertson runs the Ladies Aide Orphanage, and I am so thankful we were taken there," Esther said.

"So am I," Emma said. But her mind turned back to the baby.

"Something is bothering you now," Sam said. "What is wrong?"

"Baby Mandy is so precious. I'm sure she'll be adopted soon. Surely Mrs. Robertson will…"

"She'll make sure Mandy goes to a good home. You know that, Emma," Esther said. "We know how well she interviews potential parents. Remember, we listened outside her office one day?"

"I do remember." Emma felt a little better, but not much. That baby had worked her way into her heart, and Emma was no longer a child. "If I could adopt her, I would."

"You know that's not possible, Emma. You aren't even engaged—much less married."

"I know. But please pray that whoever adopts her will love her and take the very best care of her." Emma brushed at a tear that threatened to fall. "Let's change the subject. Do you think it might snow soon?"

Chapter 14

Emma telephoned Mrs. Robertson early the next morning to find that Mandy's teeth had come through, her fever had gone down, and she was feeling much better.

"May I stop by and see her when I get off work?"

"Of course you may, Emma. You may stop by here anytime you want, dear."

"Thank you. I'll see you this afternoon, then."

"I'll be looking for you."

Emma let Mrs. Holloway know she'd be a little late that evening and headed out to work. The wind had died down, and it was a sunny, crisp fall day. Thanksgiving would be here before they knew it, and Mrs. Holloway was adding the planning of that to all the other things she had going on.

Mary got on the trolley at her stop and took the seat Emma had saved for her. She looked quite pretty this morning, and there was a sparkle in her eyes.

"You seem to be in high spirits this morning. Did you have a good weekend?" Emma asked.

"I did. Oh Emma, the most wonderful thing happened. You know, I've told you about Edward?"

Edward was a neighbor who Mary had been sweet on for a long time. "What happened?"

"Mama asked him to Sunday dinner yesterday. At first I was so embarrassed, but Mama said it had nothing to do with me. She asked him because he's always alone and she felt sorry for him."

"And? How did it go?"

"Oh, it was wonderful. He's very easy to talk to, and he entertained us with stories about his students. He's a teacher. Did I tell you that? And he's so handsome and—"

"But what kind of man is he?"

"Very responsible, I believe. He owns his own home. It's just a few houses down from ours. And he goes to the same church we do. He asked me to a church social this coming weekend." She let out a deep sigh and smiled again.

Her smile told Emma everything she needed to know. "You said yes of course."

"I certainly did."

"I'm happy for you, Mary." And she really was. But she also felt a little envious. She wanted someone to show that kind of interest in her. And she knew who that someone was.

"Thank you, Emma. I don't know how things will progress, but I'm happy right now."

The trolley stopped, and they hurried to work. Emma was glad it was a busy Monday. It gave her less time to think about how she wished—what? What was it exactly she wanted? She wanted a home and a husband, a family of her own. But the only person who came to mind when she thought about it was Sam. And she still had problems with him being a policeman—it was a dangerous job. And he'd loved his wife dearly. Could he love another woman as much? Besides, she really didn't have any idea of how he felt about her. Did he think of her as an old friend, a little sister, or something more?

There was a look in his eyes the night before when she was holding Mandy that made her think he might have deeper feelings for her, but then again, perhaps he was thinking of Ann and the life they'd planned together.

Her board lit up in several places, and she put thoughts of Sam out of her mind for what seemed to be the hundredth time that day. She was thinking about him entirely too much lately and she needed to put a halt to it. Now.

"Operator? Are you there?"

"Yes ma'am. Whom may I connect you to?"

"No one. I just wanted to set my clock. Can you give me the correct time?"

Emma looked at the clock on the wall at the back of the room. "It's 4:35, ma'am."

"Thank you."

"You're welcome." She smiled as she disconnected the line. It still tickled her that so many people looked to her and the other operators to find out all manner of information. She was glad she liked reading the newspaper, for although it wasn't listed as a requirement, it had turned out to be a necessity to keep up with her callers' questions. And even then she couldn't answer them all.

"Good afternoon. Whom may I connect you to?" Emma asked as she plugged into a lit socket.

"Connect me to 2338."

Something about the number niggled at the back of her mind, but it wasn't until the line was connected and she heard the man on the other line say, "This is Joe," that Emma realized this was the number she'd been trying to

remember. The one where they'd been talking about stopping the meeting! She held her breath as the man she'd connected said, "I got word there's going to be another one of
those meetings in one of those nice neighborhoods. The
one we've been checking out from time to time."

"When?"

"Paper says a week from Thursday."

Emma felt sick at her stomach, and she held her breath
as she listened.

"That gives us time to plan," the man named Joe said.
"I'll be over in about an hour and we'll get it laid out."

"See you then."

Emma heard a click, and the light went out over both
lines. She committed the calling number of 2568 along
with the called number of 2338 to memory until she could
write it down, while her heart pounded so hard she could
barely catch her breath. What did she do now? Did she dare
tell her supervisor she'd been eavesdropping? She shook
her head. No. She didn't even have anything concrete to
go on unless she told what she'd overheard the last time.
It would look as if she made a habit of listening in on her
callers' conversations and she didn't.

She looked at the clock and saw that she only had a
few minutes of her shift left. Hopefully, Sam would meet
her trolley and she could tell him about it. Then she remembered that she'd miss him, but she had to check in
on Mandy. She'd have to try to call Sam later and let him
know what she'd heard. After finding out there had been
trouble after overhearing these two men's conversation
before, she had to tell someone. But what meeting were
they talking about? She must have missed something in
the morning paper. She'd have to go over it again when
she got home.

* * *

Sam hoped he didn't miss Emma. He'd stopped by Mrs. Holloway's looking for her, and found she'd planned to check on Mandy right after work but would be home for dinner.

But dark was coming earlier now, and he didn't like the idea of her traveling by herself at night. Mrs. Holloway seemed relieved that he would be seeing Emma home and invited him to have dinner with them. He gladly accepted.

He hopped on the next trolley headed for the orphanage and prayed he didn't miss Emma. It really didn't surprise him that she was checking on the baby after watching her the evening before. He hadn't been able to get the vision of her holding baby Mandy out of his mind. If anyone was meant to be a mother, he was certain it was Emma. As many children as needed parents in the city, it was a shame that a single woman couldn't adopt one. But then again, a single woman had to work for a living, and she'd have to find someone to keep the child, and that would cost her more. Besides, he felt it was better if the mother stayed at home and took care of household matters.

That's what he would want his wife to do. He wondered how Emma felt about that. Her job wasn't necessarily one a woman would want forever, at least not compared to Esther's, which was training Esther to be a pharmacist. Unless Emma wanted to go into management and become a supervisor.

He didn't really know what Emma's dreams were, but he hoped that they were to be a wife and mother one day. And he hoped he entered into her dreams as she had his.

The trolley came to a stop, and Emma stood in line to get on. The person beside Sam hurried off, and he kept his own seat, saving the one next to him for Emma.

She stepped on and he called, "Emma!"

Sam was pleased when she looked around and spotted him, a smile on her face. She looked glad to see him, but perhaps it was wishful thinking on his part and she was just happy after seeing Mandy.

But her smile held, and he felt a grin spread across his face as she stepped down the aisle and took the seat beside him.

"Sam. Where are you headed? Were you going to see Mrs. Robertson at the orphanage?"

"No. I came to escort you home. I just don't like you being out after dark by yourself."

"It's not dark yet."

"No, but it will be by the time we get back to Mrs. Holloway's. She invited me to dinner."

"Good, I was hoping to be able to talk to you this evening."

His heart slammed against his chest. "You were?"

"Yes, I overheard something that I must tell you about."

His chest deflated. Her gladness to see him had nothing to do with her feelings. "What happened?"

Emma pulled a slip of paper out of her reticule, looked around to make sure there was no one behind them, and then handed the paper to him. "The number I tried to remember before was 2338; the man answering is Joe someone—I have no idea what his last name is—and the caller is calling from 2568. Anyway, they are planning something for a meeting being held a week from this coming Thursday."

"But we don't know what meeting?"

Emma shook her head. "No. But one of the men said it was in the paper. But I don't remember seeing it in this morning's paper, and I thought I'd looked closely yesterday."

"We can look again. Do you think Mrs. Holloway will

still have yesterday's paper? If not I can try to find one. Which one does she subscribe to? I can try to get copies of yesterday's and today's."

"She takes the *Tribune* and the *Times*."

"We'll start there. If we can't find anything about a meeting on that day, I'll get some of the other papers to go through."

"All right."

"And thank you for trusting me," Sam said, his chest finally expanding again with the realization that she did trust him enough to come to him with this information. He knew she didn't like it that he was a policeman, but at least he seemed to have moved past her mistrust of *him*.

"I certainly don't want something bad to happen to anyone without doing what I can to stop it. I know I don't have much information for you to go on, but—"

"Just having the telephone numbers will help us more than you know, Emma," Sam assured her. "We can acquire the addresses from knowing those and at least find out who these men arc and put a tail on them. If you hear anything else, just let me know. That's really all you can do. And if we aren't able to stop them or find out what meeting they are talking about, it won't be your fault."

Emma let out a sigh and smiled. "Good. I couldn't bear it if something else happened at one of those meetings because I didn't tell someone what I'd heard."

"You did the right thing, Emma. Now, how is Mandy this afternoon?"

Her smile was immediate. "Oh, so much better than last night. Mrs. Robertson said her fever broke last night and hasn't come back, and those two teeth finally broke through. She was playing and smiling. But one of the other girls had to distract her while I left."

"She's become quite attached to you."

"No more than I have to her. But I think I might remind her of her mother. That is the only reason why I can see that she took such a liking to me from the very first."

"Possibly. But you are very likable, you know."

"Why, thank you, Sam."

Emma ducked her head, and Sam was sure that if it had been light enough now, he'd have seen soft color flood Emma's cheeks as she dipped her head and looked out the window.

They'd reached Emma's home by then, and Jones welcomed them both into the house. Mrs. Holloway was gracious as always, and when Emma told her about the conversations she'd heard and what they were looking for, Mrs. Holloway had Jones bring them the newspapers from that day and the day before.

"I always keep them for a couple of days in case I don't have time to read everything or need to check on something in an advertisement," Mrs. Holloway said.

"That is a very good idea, Mrs. Holloway," Sam said. "Especially today. If we can't find what we're looking for, I'll try to at least get today's copies for the other papers."

"Oh, I'm sure you'll find what you are looking for. The *Tribune* and the *Times* cover just about everything that goes on in the city."

Jones brought in the papers, and only moments later they were spread all over the parlor.

"There is notice of several women's suffrage meetings next week in the *Times*, two on Thursday," Emma said, taking the page to Sam. "I wonder which one they are talking about?"

He skimmed the notice quickly. "It won't matter. I'm sure we'll have extra coverage at both after I tell the captain."

"The notice is in the *Tribune* also. There's even notice

of the one we're holding next week," Mrs. Holloway said. She looked up at Sam. "You don't think they'd target one as small as ours, do you?"

"I would hope not, but when these kinds of people get ideas to stop a movement, they could do anything. I'll be sure to be here and see if I can get some off-duty cops to come, too. Just in case." Sam prayed there wouldn't be any problems for Mrs. Holloway's group, but it seemed that the closer these women came to gaining support, those against them stepped up their efforts to try to put an end to the meetings. "Maybe I shouldn't stay for dinner. I think I'd better go to the station to let my captain know what's going on. We need to try to find out what these men are up to as soon as we can. Thank you, Emma and Mrs. Holloway. With your help, I'm sure we can put a crimp in their plans."

"You might as well stay and eat, Sam. You have to eat anyway, and whatever it is they are planning isn't until next week. You can leave right after we eat if you need to," Emma suggested.

That's all it took to persuade him. Emma wanted him to stay. He smiled down at her. "You're right. I'll go after dinner."

She nodded. "Good. I'd hate to think you had to miss one of Mrs. Holloway's dinners."

He chuckled. "So would I."

Chapter 15

Emma was happy Sam stayed for dinner. She'd come to worry about him often. Did he get enough rest? Did he eat right when he wasn't eating with them? What did he do when he was home alone?

She didn't like to think of him being lonely, and yet, she didn't like to think there was a special woman in his life either. And she didn't know how to go about finding out. But she needed to know, because try as she might to keep caring thoughts of him out of her mind, she couldn't.

Now, as everyone said good-bye and headed toward the parlor, Emma saw Sam to the door and tried to think of a way to find out if he was interested in anyone. Or, if he was still mourning the loss of his wife.

"Will you let us know what your captain says?"

"I will."

"Good."

"Emma?"

"Yes?"

"Thank you for deciding to come to me with what you heard."

She gave a little nod. "Thanks for looking into it."

"It's my job, Emma."

"I know. And…I'm sorry I wasn't more accepting of you choosing to become a policeman at first. The department is fortunate to have you, Sam." She looked up at him and smiled. "I'm sorry if I—"

"No need to be sorry about anything, Emma. I understand why you felt that way. It did sting a bit to think you thought others might influence me. But you had good reason for mistrusting the police department."

"But I should have realized you'd never let yourself be corrupted by others. Still, to be honest, I don't love what you do. It's a dangerous job and…" She gave a little shrug.

"Emma, one can get run over walking across the street." His wife had.

"Oh Sam, I didn't mean to bring up sad memories for you."

"You didn't. But I know how quickly something like that can happen. It does make one realize how fragile life is, and it also made me want to make a difference while I'm here. Does that make any sense at all to you?"

"It does. We should all feel that way. I'm just—"

Sam placed his fingers over her lips and shook his head. "Emma, shh. None of it is your fault."

He could see the sympathy in her eyes and something more, something that had him dipping his head and capturing her lips in a brief, gentle kiss. He raised his head and looked into her eyes. For a second he'd thought he felt her respond, but she quickly ended the kiss and took a step back. Sam was thankful that she didn't seem to take offense.

In fact, she didn't seem to know what to say, and he decided it might be time to leave. "I'll let you know what the captain says."

She nodded and let out what sounded like a shaky breath, and Sam wondered if she'd been as affected by the quick kiss as he had been. "All right. Take care, Sam."

He smiled at her and gave her chin a little nudge. "I always do, Emma. Try not to worry. The Lord has me covered."

Emma had just about given up hearing from Sam when the telephone rang. She didn't wait for Jones to come to the parlor, hurrying into the foyer instead.

"No sir. She's right here, Mr. Tucker," Jones said as he saw Emma. He handed the receiver to her. "Mr. Tucker for you, Miss Emma."

"Thank you, Jones." She took the receiver from him and put her ear to the earpiece. "Sam?"

"Emma, I was just asking Jones if it was too late to speak with you. But I had a feeling you'd be pacing the floor waiting to hear what the captain said."

"You were right. What *did* he say?"

"He's quite pleased with the information. We've already got the addresses for both numbers and have men staking them out. This Joe person—his last name is Parker, by the way—has been arrested on numerous occasions and just got out of jail a few months ago. But we think the other guy—a Frank Carson—is the ringleader of a small gang that's working for someone else. At any rate, we know who to look for, and if you hear anything more, please telephone me immediately. If you can't get hold of me, ask for Captain Miller."

Emma's heart flooded with relief that she'd done the right thing by telling Sam. "I will."

"I know you will. And Emma, try to get some sleep. If we can't stop them from causing trouble, it's not going to be your fault."

"Thank you, Sam."

"Thank *you*, Emma. You've been a great help to us. I'll speak to you tomorrow. And oh, I was wondering…"

Emma caught her breath a moment. "Yes?"

"Would you like to go to church with me on Sunday? I've been telling Ann's parents about you helping with my plan at the orphanage, and they'd like to meet you."

Emma wasn't sure what to say. Ann's parents? Did she really want to meet them? Then again, how could she decline gracefully? "Yes, I'll go to church with you."

"Good. I'm glad," Sam said. "I'll talk to you more about it tomorrow and let you go get some rest. You'll tell the others what the captain said?"

"I will."

" 'Night, Emma."

"Good night, Sam."

Emma put the receiver back in its holder and released a breath. All thought of the conversation she'd overheard and the captain's reaction to it was forgotten for the moment, her thoughts spinning over Sam's invitation.

"Emma?" Esther peeked her head out of the parlor. "Was that Sam?"

Emma nodded and hurried back to the parlor to tell them all what Sam had said about the captain. The rest she kept to herself, at least for now.

Sam sat staring at the telephone at the police station. Emma had agreed to go to church with him and meet Ann's parents. She had no way of knowing what a huge step he'd just taken. He hadn't intended to ask her to go to church with him, but after kissing her—brief as it was—he hadn't been able to get her out of his mind.

He cared deeply about this woman, and there was no more denying it or evading it. He wanted to declare his love for her from the rooftops of the city, but he wasn't sure she was ready to hear him just yet.

While she might finally trust him, she still didn't like his profession, and she might not be willing to marry a policeman under any circumstances—not even if she loved him. His heart seemed to come to a standstill at that thought, and yet it didn't keep him from loving her.

And he wanted her to meet Ann's parents because they were part of his life and would be in hers, too, if he were so blessed as to win her heart and marry her.

But Sam didn't feel he could declare his love for Emma just yet. It felt too soon. He'd just won her trust, or thought he had. But that didn't mean she felt as deeply about him as he did her. Although he was almost certain she'd responded—however lightly—to his kiss, and he hoped with everything in him that he hadn't imagined that she had. Still, even if she did, she deserved to be courted, and if things went as he hoped they would this Sunday, he prayed she would let him do just that.

He headed to his apartment and tried to get his mind off that kiss. The captain had been pleased with the information Emma had come up with. And he'd told Sam to be sure to attend any meetings at the Holloway house, just in case there was trouble there.

"Many of these groups have begun to spread out from the larger meetings to the smaller ones, hoping to put a stop to more groups forming. I think these people are being paid by someone or by another group, and it's very hard to find out who is really organizing it all," the captain had said. "It's possible that Frank Carson is the contact person for whoever that is, but it remains to be seen."

Sam prayed that none of those smaller groups decided to visit Mrs. Holloway's meeting. He'd talk to Andrew and Jones about it to make sure they would watch out for any strangers casing the area. They'd do all they could to find these thugs, and he hoped they'd get information that would lead them to the real ringleaders.

"Lord, please watch over the Holloway house and all of those in it, especially Emma. You already know how much I've come to love her, Father, and I pray that it's Your will that she might love me back. But if not, please help me to deal with the hurt and go on. You've been with me through all kinds of loss—and I pray that Emma won't be another one—but I know that You will be with me come what may. Please keep her safe. In Jesus' name I pray, amen."

Emma woke with a smile on her face the next morning. Sam had kissed her last night, and he'd asked her to go to church with him. Surely that meant he cared about her more than just as a friend who would help out with his plan. Or did it? Maybe it only meant that he considered her a very good friend. And she wanted him to feel that way. She wanted his friendship as well.

But something *had* changed between them last night, and it had started with that kiss. Brief as it might have been. It was tender and sweet, and Emma knew that all the warnings she'd given herself about falling in love with Sam had been for naught. Her heart was his whether he wanted it or not. *Oh dear Lord, please let him want it. But if not, please help me to deal with it and find a way to remain friends with him.*

For now she tried to put thoughts of romance out of her

mind as she got ready for work. She hurried down to breakfast and found that everyone else had beaten her down.

"Running late today, Emma?" Grace asked. Grace was usually the last one down, as everyone else had to be at work before she needed to go.

"I must be." But she wasn't going to let her little sister get on her nerves this morning. "Either that or you're early."

"Emma dear, I'm so glad Sam has been coming to our meetings and will be at the next one. I've thought about canceling it but I really don't think we're in any danger, do you?"

"I don't know, Mrs. Holloway. I hope not. Maybe Sam can advise us about it."

"I don't want to cancel it if we don't need to. Hopefully the police will be somewhere around should we need them."

"I'm sure that Sam will make sure this place is watched the night of the meeting," Andrew said.

"I think so, too. Hopefully, those troublemakers will be somewhere else that night. Before they were talking about it being a 'big' meeting," Emma said. "We aren't that large a group. Surely they won't target us."

"I'll check with Sam and see what he thinks we should do. I certainly don't want anyone who comes to a meeting here injured. But I don't want to let thugs stop our cause either," Mrs. Holloway said.

"Sam will let us know what we should do," Emma said, trusting his judgment. "He knows how important the movement is to us all. You can make your decision after you talk to him."

Chapter 16

The rest of the week passed quickly and uneventfully. Emma heard no more calls from the two men to each other—at least not to the numbers she'd given Sam. And she was sure she'd recognize those two voices now even if they came from another telephone number. Sam had advised Mrs. Holloway not to change her plans unless that was what she wanted to do. He would be there and the house would be surrounded while the meeting was going on.

But Emma had more on her mind than those callers or what might happen at the women's suffrage meeting. Each day she became a little more nervous about meeting Sam's late wife's parents. And yet, she knew those two people were very important to Sam. He loved them, and whether he ever remarried or not, he would want his wife to care about them, too. He wouldn't just desert them for the woman he loved, and it would make it hard on a marriage if she didn't accept them as being part of his life. They were family to him.

Of course, she was jumping way ahead of herself even thinking about it. Sam hadn't given any indication that he was thinking of marrying again and certainly not to her. They'd shared a kiss, but that didn't mean he was on the verge of asking to court her—much less asking her to marry him.

But when Sunday arrived, she admitted to herself that was exactly what she wanted—she loved him. And while she did not want to come in second to Ann, she wanted a life with Sam. *Dear Lord, please help me to accept it if that is not what Sam wants. And please let me know soon how he feels about me.*

She'd only told everyone she was attending church with Sam the evening before. And she'd tried to make it sound as casual as she could. Evidently she succeeded, because not even Grace questioned her about it, saying only, "Good. Maybe he'll come with you one day."

Now as she headed downstairs her stomach felt as if a bevy of butterflies had been released, and she was glad she hadn't eaten this morning.

Sam had telephoned the evening before to let her know when to expect him, and he arrived right on time.

They said their good-byes to everyone else and caught the trolley that would take them to Sam's church. She hoped Sam couldn't tell how anxious she was about meeting the Brisbanes.

But as if he could read her mind, he covered one of her hands with his. "There's nothing to be nervous about. They will love you, and I think you'll feel the same about them. I hope you don't mind, but they've asked us to come for Sunday dinner and I told them we would."

Emma bit her bottom lip. She wasn't sure she was

ready to meet Ann's parents, let alone spend the afternoon with them.

"I did tell them that we would as long as you didn't have somewhere else to be. So we don't have to, but…"

Emma could tell he wanted to say more and she prodded, "But what?"

"You are very special to me, Emma. And so are they. Whether any of you like each other or not, you will remain special to me and so will they. I just wanted you to meet each other. But we don't have go to Sunday dinner if you'd rather not."

She couldn't bring herself to say the words she wanted to. She couldn't disappoint him. She turned her gloved hand over in his and gave his fingers a gentle squeeze. "It's all right. We'll go to Sunday dinner."

Mr. and Mrs. Brisbane were waiting for them outside the church building. Emma could tell they were as nervous as she was. Meeting a woman friend of Sam's and knowing he was getting on with his life couldn't be easy for them, even if Sam said they were only friends. Her heart flooded with compassion for them, and she smiled as Sam made the introductions.

"We're so glad you could join us today, Miss Chapman."

"Thank you. Sam thinks so highly of you both, I'm glad to meet you. Thank you for your invitation to Sunday dinner, Mrs. Brisbane. That's very nice of you." Emma didn't want her worrying all through church that she might have told Sam she didn't want to go.

The woman smiled at Emma and slipped an arm through hers. "Thank you, Miss Chapman. For being willing to come."

Emma suddenly knew they both understood that each of them cared for Sam and that everything was going to be all right. The invitation had been offered out of love for Sam. And it'd been accepted for the very same reason. They were going to get along just fine.

She liked the church, and the minister preached a good sermon on trust. Something she needed to hear. She had learned to trust Sam, and now she needed to trust that the Lord had both of their best interests at heart. Whatever happened between her and Sam, she needed to trust that He was in control and He'd be with them both.

Mr. and Mrs. Brisbane introduced her to their many friends, and by the time they got to the Brisbane home, Emma knew that she would be made to feel comfortable there. But it was when she was helping Mrs. Brisbane with the dessert in the kitchen that she understood fully why Sam loved these two people as much as he did.

Emma was dishing up ice cream to go along with the cherry pie she'd learned was Sam's favorite. As Mrs. Brisbane put a huge slice on a plate, she said, "I'll be glad to give you the recipe, dear."

"Why, thank you. I don't do much cooking living with Mrs. Holloway. I suppose it's something I should think about doing more though."

"Sam does like to eat," Mrs. Holloway said with a twinkling eye. "So you might think about it before you get married."

"Married?"

"Emma, if Sam asked you to come to meet us, he's planning on marrying you. He wouldn't have brought you here if that wasn't the case."

Emma's heart began to hammer against her chest, and she covered her mouth. "I—"

"You love him very much, don't you?" Mrs. Brisbane asked. "You don't need to answer. I can see it in both of you—the way you look at each other. I just want you to know that we want you as part of this family." Tears filled the woman's eyes as she continued. "I only had one child, but I'd love to think I could have another daughter."

Emma wiped at her eyes. "Oh Mrs. Brisbane. You are right. I do love Sam. But I'm not totally sure how he feels about me. But I would be honored to be considered part of your family under any circumstances—whether Sam and I are just friends or more."

The two women hugged each other until Mr. Brisbane called out, "What's holding up dessert? Do you need any help in there?"

Both women wiped their tears and smiled at each other. "No, dear. We're bringing it out now."

Once she and Sam had taken a seat on the trolley, Sam turned to her. "Thank you. They like you very much. I could tell."

"I like them a lot, too. Thank you for taking me to meet them. I can see why you love them so much."

"They are very special to me. And so are you."

Emma's heart slammed against her chest as she waited for him to continue. "I think I fell in love with them as much as I did Ann. And now I've loved them longer."

Emma's heart broke all over again for Sam and the Brisbanes' loss.

"But I've known you longer than any of them, Emma, and I...I've come to care a great deal about the woman you've become. I'd like to court you if you think you might be—"

"Sam, I would be glad to be courted by you."

He grinned. "Even though I'm a policeman?"

She let out an exaggerated sigh. "I suppose. I seem to have gotten past my initial shock."

"I'm glad you have."

He grinned at her and looked at her in a way that set her pulse racing. "So am I."

"Should I ask permission of Mrs. Holloway?"

"I don't believe so. I'll tell her you've asked to court me and I've said you may. She'll be happy about it, I'm certain."

"What about Grace?"

"I don't need her permission, Sam."

He threw back his head and laughed. "I certainly hope not. But do you think she'll be happy?"

"Oh, I don't know. I think she's a little sweet on you herself, but she'll come around. And actually, I think she'll take credit for it." Emma chuckled, her heart full of love for Sam.

He nodded. "She might just do that."

Chapter 17

Jones opened the door for them, and they hurried to the parlor where they knew a warm fire awaited them. Everyone greeted them with enthusiasm, and Sam was glad to see Mr. Collins there also. Maybe he wouldn't have to stand out in the cold to wait for the trolley tonight.

Sam still couldn't believe Emma had said he could court her. Of course, it didn't mean that she'd say yes to a marriage proposal—only that he could pursue her, that they could spend more time together to see if that outcome were possible.

He seemed to have her trust, but could he get her past her fear that something would happen to him? He prayed he could.

"My, it must be cold out. Your faces are rosy as can be."

Sam and Emma both turned to face the fireplace, and he flashed a smile at her. Was it the cold or the fact that she'd agreed to let him court her that had their faces flushed even in front of the fire?

"It is getting colder out. The fire feels real good."

"How was your afternoon?" Mrs. Holloway asked.

"It was very enjoyable," Emma said. "The Brisbanes are extremely nice and made me feel quite comfortable."

To Sam, it seemed Mrs. Holloway visibly relaxed. She'd probably worried about Emma all afternoon. That she loved the girls was obvious, and he was glad they had this woman in their lives. He was sure they loved her as much as he loved the Brisbanes.

"Good. I'm glad you had a nice time."

"I believe it's going to snow soon," Sam said.

"I wouldn't be a bit surprised," Andrew affirmed.

"Pretty as it is though, I do dread working in it," Sam said.

"I wish you didn't have to," Emma said.

He grinned down at her. "It's not all that bad. And one benefit to it is that not a lot of criminals like to work in it either. Trudging around in the snow can leave footprints."

"I suppose I never thought of that," Emma said.

Sam leaned nearer. "Oh, I'm teasing you, Emma. But I would think before I got out in bad weather if I had a choice, but I suppose some criminals might think it's the perfect time to commit a crime."

During Sunday night supper, Andrew and Esther reported on their visit at the orphanage.

"You should have seen Margaret's face when we told her we wanted to help her. Be a benefactor to her as Mrs. Holloway has been to me. We told her in Mrs. Robertson's office. She was so happy, and we are so pleased to be able to help her," Esther said.

"And we hired Betsy as a receptionist," Andrew said.

"She'll work part-time until school is out and then full-time."

"So, it seems they'll all have jobs by this summer. That's such a big relief. Now all we have to do is help them find places to live, and that shouldn't be too hard," Emma said, turning to Sam. "Your idea has already helped them so much, Sam!"

"It couldn't have happened without all of you. But it is encouraging—for us as well as for them." And it was wonderful news, but tonight it came in second to the fact that the woman beside him said he could court her. *Thank You, Lord.*

Mr. Collins did offer him a ride home, and as much as he wanted a few minutes with Emma, he knew she wouldn't want him to turn down a ride home. However, it really didn't hinder them having a moment alone because it seemed Mr. Collins and Mrs. Holloway wanted the same thing.

Sam couldn't help but grin when, just as they were about to leave, Mr. Collins said, "Oh Miriam, I forgot to get that book I wanted to borrow from you."

"I'm sorry. Come on into the study and I'll get it for you."

Sam didn't waste a moment as the couple turned and went in the other direction. He quickly pulled Emma into the dining room and looked down into her eyes. "I thought I wasn't going to be able to talk to you alone before I left. I know we don't have much time, but I have to know."

"Know what, Sam?"

"Did you really say I could court you?"

Her smile answered him before her words did. "I did do that, didn't I?"

"And you meant it?"

"I did. Is it all right if I tell everyone or—"

"Since you didn't say anything, I thought maybe you'd changed your mind."

"Oh no. I didn't change my mind. I think I just wanted time to believe you want to court me. But we can go tell them now, if you like." She pulled on his hand to lead him back to the parlor.

He pulled her back into the dining room. "No, you tell them whenever you want and however you want. I just needed reassurance from you."

"You have it." And then she stood on tiptoe and kissed his cheek.

Only the footsteps he heard in the foyer kept Sam from pulling Emma into his arms and really kissing her. They eased out of the dining room just as Andrew and Esther reached the doorway.

"Oh Sam, I'm glad you haven't left yet," Andrew said. "You know, I've been meaning to ask you something and was going to last Sunday night, but we were called out with baby Mandy."

"What is it, Andrew?"

"I was wondering if you'd consider being my best man? I know it's kind of late and all, but I'd really be honored if you'd stand up with me."

"I'll be glad to stand with you, Andrew." Sam grinned. It had been one great day. "I'm the one who is honored. Thank you for asking me."

Mrs. Holloway, Mr. Collins, and Grace all joined them in the foyer just as Esther said, "You'll be Emma's partner. She's the maid of honor of course."

Sam's glance slid to Emma, and he smiled. "I can't think of anyone I'd rather be a partner with."

When she giggled, Esther asked, "Is there something you two wish to tell us?"

"I don't know." Emma turned to him and grinned. "Is there, Sam?"

He took her smile and her words as permission to say, "There is. It's been a wonderful day. And I'm happy to stand up with you. But the very best thing that happened today is that Emma has given me permission to court her."

"I knew it! I knew it. I planned this from the beginning!" Grace said.

Sam and Emma looked at each other and chuckled. Of course she did.

Chapter 18

Emma hurried to work the next day, eager to get it over with so she could see Sam again.

Everyone had seemed very happy about Sam courting her, including Mrs. Holloway. "I had a suspicion that was the way things were headed when Sam wanted to introduce you to Ann's parents," she'd said just before Emma left that morning.

"I must admit, I had hopes, but I really didn't know. I do understand why he loves them so much. They..." Tears came to Emma's eyes remembering Mrs. Brisbane's words to her. "He's a son to them, and if he asks me to marry him, they will welcome me into their family just as you will welcome Sam."

"If?" Esther had said. "Oh Emma. The man is totally in love with you. We've all seen it coming for weeks."

"You have?"

"Of course we have," Grace had added. "You've been stealing looks at each other for weeks now."

Emma had let out a deep sigh and smiled. "*I'm* still having a hard time believing he asked to court me. I'll take it one step at a time."

Now, as Mary got on the trolley, Emma debated telling her, but Mary was full of her own news and Emma decided to wait to share hers.

"Oh Emma, I think I'm in love."

"I take it things are going quite well with Edward?"

"They seem to be. He's asked to take me to dinner this next weekend. And he's sitting by me at church."

"That sounds very promising." Emma wondered if she looked as happy as Mary did. After all, Sam had actually asked to court her—she had to tell herself that over and over and hoped that she truly would believe it one day.

"I certainly hope so. Mama expects him to propose any day now."

"I'm happy for you, Mary."

"Thank you, Emma. It just shows we can't give up. You'll find someone one of these days, too."

Emma only smiled. She already had. But she'd hold that news close to her heart for a while longer.

Now that Emma was so anxious to get home, instead of speeding by as most workdays did, this one seemed to drag on and on and on. By the time she left for the day, she couldn't wait to get on the trolley in hopes that Sam would be waiting for her at her stop.

But she was very disappointed when he wasn't there. Had he changed his mind about wanting to court her? Her heart plummeted deeper and deeper as she made her way home.

Jones opened the door for her, and even he seemed to

notice her mood had changed drastically from that morning. "Are you all right, Miss Emma?"

The telephone rang just then, and Grace yelled, "I'll get it, Jones!"

Since she had friends calling from time to time, she'd taken to answering it when she was nearby. From the look on Jones's face, he thought she was encroaching on his duties. But anyone could tell that he was crazy about Grace, and he gave Emma a tight smile now. "She said she was expecting a call."

Emma only nodded and headed toward the parlor.

"Emma!" Grace said as she passed by her. She held the receiver out to her. "Your love is calling!"

"Grace!" But at her words, Emma's heart suddenly began to pound, louder and harder, with each step she took. She placed the earpiece to her ear and said, "Hello?"

"Emma? That Grace. But you know, she's right. You are my love. At least I certainly want you to be."

Relief washed over Emma as she sank down onto the small chair next to the telephone table. "Oh Sam. I didn't know what to think when you didn't meet my trolley. I thought maybe you'd changed your mind."

"Oh, I'm not going to change my mind. But I am upset."

"Why?"

"I've been called in on evening duty for the rest of the week. One of the officers came down sick, and it means I'm not going to get to see you until Thursday evening. I will get to come to that because I'll be on duty for it. I just wanted to hear your voice and let you know why you wouldn't be seeing me for a few days."

"Oh Sam. I'm disappointed, but I understand." She was going to have to understand these changes in his work schedule if they were going to be seeing more of each other and if it led to him asking her to marry him. She needed to accept it and try to be as understanding as she could.

"Thank you, Emma. I'll try to telephone you about this time tomorrow, too."

"Oh, good. Sam, be careful out there."

"I will. And Emma, always remember the Lord has me covered."

Peace settled over her at his words. Oh, she knew he wasn't saying he'd never get hurt, but that come what may, he trusted that the Lord would be there. She needed to do the same thing.

Sam couldn't wait to get to Mrs. Holloway's for the meeting. It'd been three and a half long days without seeing Emma, and talking to her over the telephone wasn't enough.

At least he didn't have to pretend he wasn't on duty tonight. He prayed there would be no trouble, but they'd been able to tap into the lines of the numbers Emma had given him, and today the name Holloway had been mentioned as one of the meetings they were targeting along with several larger ones. A number of policemen were being sent out to all of them, and Sam knew that there would be at least five out around Mrs. Holloway's home watching for trouble.

But he would speak to Andrew and Jones—and Mr. Collins if he were there. They needed to be on guard, too. He hadn't decided if he should tell Emma and the other women just yet, and as he took the steps up to Mrs. Holloway's front door, he sent up a prayer for the Lord to look after them all tonight.

He arrived early so that he could see everyone who came, and he knew Jones would let him know if anyone suspicious came in. The butler opened the door just as Sam reached the top step, and his heart did some kind of funny twist as he saw Emma coming toward him from the parlor.

"Sam! You came a little early. I'm so glad!"

He grasped her outstretched hand—although he would have loved to pull her into his arms.

"Is there anywhere we can talk privately for a moment?" he whispered.

She smiled then led him into the study and away from Jones and any early arrivers.

"I've missed seeing you!" she said.

"And I've missed you. I should have waited a week to ask to court you when I actually could," he replied.

"Oh no. I'm glad you asked when you did. But I will be glad when this week is over."

"So will I." He gazed down into her eyes, and then his glance slid to her lips. Oh, how he wanted to kiss her. He dipped his head—

"Emma, where are you?"

Grace. Of course. Sam lifted his head and stepped back. He shook his head and smiled. Was that disappointment he saw in Emma's eyes? He was certain she could see it in his.

"Call her in. I need to tell you both something anyway," he whispered.

"In here, Emma. Sam has something he wants to tell us."

"All of us?" Grace asked as she entered the study.

"All the family, Jones, and Mr. Collins, too, if he's here," Sam said.

In only a moment, everyone had gathered in the study—including Jones. "I wanted to alert you all that this meeting may be targeted tonight. We don't really know, but there are policemen outside, ready to help if there is any trouble. I don't think there is a need to mention it to your guests at this time, but you all mean a great deal to me and I felt I should let you know before the others start arriving."

"I never heard anything from those numbers today," Emma said. "I would have told you if I had."

"I believe you. Actually we've had the line tapped, but your supervisor took the calls—we'd alerted the telephone company—and she let us know, too."

"It must have been when she relieved me for lunch," Emma said.

"I'm glad you didn't intercept them and that I could tell you."

She nodded. "So am I."

"Just try to stay calm. Jones, you'll let us know if anyone suspicious tries to get in?"

"I will, sir."

"All right. Don't worry. I do know the men who will be outside, and I'm armed even though I'm not in uniform. We didn't want to tip their hand. Just act like normal."

The doorbell rang signaling the first guests, and Jones hurried to answer the door.

"Go on and do what you need to," Sam said to Emma. "I'm hoping we'll get a few moments to ourselves after the meeting."

Emma nodded. "So am I."

The women went to greet their guests and Sam, Andrew, and Mr. Collins stayed behind. Andrew shut the study door and turned to Sam. "Tell us what you'll want us to do if there should be any problems."

"Just do what you'd do naturally. Protect our women the best you can. Get them out of the line of fire if there is any. It might be better if you sit a little nearer to them tonight. I'll be in the back hoping to stop anything before it happens. And pray."

Chapter 19

Emma didn't want to sit in the front as usual. She wanted to sit in the back beside Sam, but she knew without asking that he wouldn't allow it, not tonight. She prayed for nothing bad to happen and for the Lord to keep them all safe, but she knew she wouldn't relax until the meeting was over and she and Sam could have a few moments alone.

Mrs. Lila Chesterfield was the speaker tonight and as hard as Emma tried, she couldn't concentrate on a word she was saying. She knew Sam would put his life on the line tonight if he had to, and now she wished she'd ignored Grace's call and just kissed him.

The meeting seemed to drag on just as the week at work had until suddenly there was what sounded like a scuffle outside the door, a thud against it, and then it burst open—and two men brandishing guns ran into the room.

"Get down, ladies!" Andrew yelled, pulling Esther and Emma down at the same time. She saw that Mr. Collins had grabbed Mrs. Holloway and Grace, pushing them down, too. And then gunshots rang out, and Emma turned to see Sam with his gun pulled. She yanked out of Andrew's grasp and, feeling like her body moved as though mired by mud, tried to hurry to Sam's side, but watched as the man in the doorway slumped against the door and aimed his gun at Sam. Blasts exploded from both guns.

"Sam!" she yelled as she reached his side. He held his side while blood seeped through his fingers. He slipped to the floor, and she dropped down beside him. He turned white, his shirt darkening with blood. "Sam! Sam, don't you dare die on me now!"

Policemen swarmed into the room, and only then did Emma see that there were two gunmen on the floor. Blood seemed to be everywhere.

Andrew appeared at her side and began checking Sam out.

"He's obviously been shot, but I think it was a clean one. I'm sure he's going to be all right, Emma." He handed her a handkerchief out of his pocket, and Emma realized that tears were streaming down her face. "We'll get him to the hospital and get him fixed up. Until then, press this cloth against his wound. It looks like Jones got hurt, too," Andrew continued as Esther rushed to his side.

Everything from that point on was a blur to Emma until they were all at the hospital waiting to hear how Sam and Jones were. Emma and Esther rode to the hospital with Andrew and Sam in the ambulance. Mrs. Holloway, Grace, and Mr. Collins had waited until all the guests were accounted for and the policemen had filled them in on everything. Several officers remained there to tie things up.

"Oh, I wish I'd have canceled the meeting," Mrs. Holloway said, dabbing at her tear-filled eyes. "Sam and Jones were both heroes tonight."

"Was Jones shot, too?" Emma asked, realizing she didn't know exactly what had happened to him.

"No. But one of the gunmen hit him hard enough with the butt of his gun that he was knocked out and bleeding."

"Oh, poor Jones."

"I'm sure Andrew will come out as soon as he can to let us know how they are," Esther said.

Emma rocked back and forth in her seat, and Grace hurried over to hug her. "Sam is going to be all right, Emma. I'm sure he is."

Emma could only nod and rock some more. Mrs. Holloway dropped down into the seat beside her and pulled her into a hug. "It's going to be all right, Emma dear."

Emma couldn't hold back her tears any longer. "And if he is—oh Mrs. Holloway, I'm not sure I can face living with fear that he might be killed every time he leaves me," she whispered. "I'm so scared."

"Oh my dear Emma. I know that you've had much loss in your lifetime, but none of us can guarantee one more minute in this life—no matter where we are or where we work. A stray bullet could hit Sam on a day off. Do you really want to live your life without Sam's love, on the chance that you might lose him?"

Emma swallowed around the knot in her throat and shook her head.

"What possible good would that do?" Mrs. Holloway continued. "I can tell you now, I lost my husband much sooner than I wanted to, but I would not give up one day, one hour, not one minute I spent with him. You know firsthand that the Lord is always there to get you through whatever comes in this life, Emma. He brought you and Sam together. Are you really going to turn away the love God set in your path?"

No. She was going to trust, as she'd made up her mind

only a few days ago to do. Trust that Sam would be all right. Trust that they would have a life together. And trust in the Lord to get them through it all.

Sam opened his eyes and groaned. Where was he? What happened—Emma! Was she all right? He rose up and the room spun.

"Hey, take it easy, Sam." Andrew's arm stopped his movements, and he lowered him back to the bed. "Emma is all right, if that's what you're worrying about. You stopped what could have been a tragic ending to the evening, Sam. And you'll live to tell about it."

Only then did Sam release his pent-up breath. "I got shot?"

Andrew chuckled. "You did. But it was a clean shot and didn't hit any organs. You won't be working for a while, but you'll be fine."

"Jones? I saw him fall just as the men stormed the room."

"He was trying to stop them—evidently the other policemen didn't get there quite quick enough. But thankfully, they didn't shoot him. He's going to have one awful headache for a few days, but he'll be fine, too."

"And everyone else is all right?"

"Everyone is fine. Or will be once I let them know you and Jones are, too. I'm assuming you'd like to see Emma?"

"Yes."

"I'll go get her."

Sam leaned back against his pillow and began praying. "Thank You, Lord, that Emma and the others are all okay, and that Jones and I are, too. Lord, I'm afraid this might make Emma change her mind about me. I know I have her trust now, but I know how badly she hates this job I have. I don't know if she'll be willing to marry me with the fear she's bound to have now. And yet, I feel this job is something I must do. But Lord, if I'm wrong about that, please let me know. I don't want to lose Emma, I—"

"Sam?"

He opened his eyes and saw the woman he loved standing at the door, her eyes full of tears. She brought up a hand to brush at them.

"I'm sorry for worrying you, Emma."

A sob broke from her chest as she rushed over to him. "Oh Sam. *I'm* sorry. I—I overheard your prayer just now, and I'm sorry I made you feel I wouldn't love you enough to accept that you are doing a job you feel called to do. You were a hero tonight. You saved lives. There is no way I'd ask you to quit. I'm just going to have to trust that God has you covered."

"Oh Emma. Does that mean—"

"I think it means we could have a short courtship, if you—"

"You'll marry me?"

Emma bent down and placed a hand on each side of his face. "Oh yes, Sam Tucker. I will marry you. And the sooner, the better."

Sam chuckled, put a hand on her neck, and pulled her face closer. "Sounds good to me."

Emma pressed her lips against his, and together they sealed the promise of love for a lifetime.

Epilogue

Esther and Andrew insisted that Emma and Sam share their wedding day with a double wedding. They quickly agreed—not wanting Mrs. Holloway to have to plan one wedding right after another.

Now, only a week before Christmas, Emma followed Esther down the garland-draped staircase and into the parlor. She took her place alongside Esther as she and Andrew said their vows, and stole glances at her husband-to-be. Sam had never looked so handsome as he did now. His wink had her blushing as she tried to give her attention to the vows Andrew and Esther were taking. As soon as the couple shared their first kiss as husband and wife, they exchanged places with Emma and Sam.

Emma felt blessed in so many ways. Mr. Collins sat between Mrs. Holloway and Grace, and Emma was almost certain there would be another wedding around Valentine's Day. She hoped so. Mrs. Holloway deserved to have a love of her own.

Mrs. Holloway had gone out of her way to make this day special for her and Sam, too, inviting Mr. and Mrs. Brisbane, several of her and Sam's coworkers, and for them all, Mrs. Robertson and all the young people they'd been helping.

And Mrs. Robertson had even brought baby Mandy. Tears gathered in Emma's eyes just thinking of Sam's wedding present to her. He'd already talked to Mrs. Robertson, and all the paperwork was ready for them to fill out to adopt the baby once they signed the marriage certificate and Emma was officially Mrs. Samuel Tucker.

It would take a few weeks for all the paperwork to go through—just long enough for them to get settled in their new apartment after their wedding trip, Mrs. Robertson said—and then Mandy would be theirs.

Now, as she and Sam exchanged their vows before the Lord and all their family and friends, and their daughter-to-be, Emma sent up a prayer of thanksgiving to the Lord above for bringing this hero of a man into her life. She was going to trust Him to always have them covered.

* * * * *

REQUEST YOUR FREE BOOKS!
2 FREE RIVETING INSPIRATIONAL NOVELS
PLUS 2 FREE MYSTERY GIFTS

YES! Please send me 2 FREE Love Inspired® Suspense novels and my 2 FREE mystery gifts (gifts are worth about $10). After receiving them, if I don't wish to receive any more books, I can return the shipping statement marked "cancel." If I don't cancel, I will receive 4 brand-new novels every month and be billed just $4.49 per book in the U.S. or $4.99 per book in Canada. That's a savings of at least 22% off the cover price. It's quite a bargain! Shipping and handling is just 50¢ per book in the U.S. and 75¢ per book in Canada.* I understand that accepting the 2 free books and gifts places me under no obligation to buy anything. I can always return a shipment and cancel at any time. Even if I never buy another book, the two free books and gifts are mine to keep forever.

123/323 IDN FVZV

Name   (PLEASE PRINT)

Address   Apt. #

City   State/Prov.   Zip/Postal Code

Signature (if under 18, a parent or guardian must sign)

Mail to the Harlequin® Reader Service:
IN U.S.A.: P.O. Box 1867, Buffalo, NY 14240-1867
IN CANADA: P.O. Box 609, Fort Erie, Ontario L2A 5X3

**Are you a subscriber to Love Inspired Suspense
and want to receive the larger-print edition?
Call 1-800-873-8635 or visit www.ReaderService.com.**

LISDIR13

REQUEST YOUR FREE BOOKS!

2 FREE INSPIRATIONAL NOVELS
PLUS 2
FREE
MYSTERY GIFTS

Love Inspired
HISTORICAL
INSPIRATIONAL HISTORICAL ROMANCE

YES! Please send me 2 FREE Love Inspired® Historical novels and my 2 FREE mystery gifts (gifts are worth about $10). After receiving them, if I don't wish to receive any more books, I can return the shipping statement marked "cancel." If I don't cancel, I will receive 4 brand-new novels every month and be billed just $4.49 per book in the U.S. or $4.99 per book in Canada. That's a savings of at least 22% off the cover price. It's quite a bargain! Shipping and handling is just 50¢ per book in the U.S. and 75¢ per book in Canada.* I understand that accepting the 2 free books and gifts places me under no obligation to buy anything. I can always return a shipment and cancel at any time. Even if I never buy another book, the two free books and gifts are mine to keep forever.

102/302 IDN FV2V

Name	(PLEASE PRINT)
Address	Apt. #
City	State/Prov. Zip/Postal Code

Signature (if under 18, a parent or guardian must sign)

Mail to the Harlequin® Reader Service:
IN U.S.A.: P.O. Box 1867, Buffalo, NY 14240-1867
IN CANADA: P.O. Box 609, Fort Erie, Ontario L2A 5X3

Want to try two free books from another series?
Call 1-800-873-8635 or visit www.ReaderService.com.

* Terms and prices subject to change without notice. Prices do not include applicable taxes. Sales tax applicable in N.Y. Canadian residents will be charged applicable taxes. Offer not valid in Quebec. This offer is limited to one order per household. Not valid for current subscribers to Love Inspired Historical books. All orders subject to credit approval. Credit or debit balances in a customer's account(s) may be offset by any other outstanding balance owed by or to the customer. Please allow 4 to 6 weeks for delivery. Offer available while quantities last.

LIHDIR13

HEARTSONG
PRESENTS

Look out for 4 new
Heartsong Presents books next month!

**Every month 4 inspiring faith-filled
romances will be available in stores.**

These contemporary and historical Christian
romances emphasize God's role in every
relationship and reinforce the importance of
faith, hope and love.

RB   LB
  JL.B SB
  mini
    CB
DB